"What a pair we are. Special things are worth waiting for, or however that saying goes." David laughed.

"You might regain your memory before we're able to—" Patty started.

"Shh. We're living in the moment, remember? And in this moment at hand I'm going to kiss you again before Sarah Ann and Tucker wake up from their naps."

"Good idea."

The kiss ignited all the heat and passion of the one before, but now there was more. There was a sense of anticipation of what was yet to come intertwined with the desire.

There was a depth of understanding, of rightness, of knowing they would cherish this gift they had given themselves, and the memories of all they would share. They were in a place where neither of them had been before.

And it was good.

Dear Reader,

Well, June may be the traditional month for weddings, but we here at Silhouette find June is busting out all over—with babies! We begin with Christine Rimmer's *Fifty Ways To Say I'm Pregnant*. When bound-for-the-big-city Starr Bravo shares a night of passion with the rancher she's always loved, she finds herself in the family way. But how to tell him? *Fifty Ways* is a continuation of Christine's Bravo Family saga, so look for the BRAVO FAMILY TIES flash. And for those of you who remember Christine's JONES GANG series, you'll be delighted with the cameo appearance of an old friend....

Next, Joan Elliott Pickart continues her miniseries THE BABY BET: MacALLISTER'S GIFTS with *Accidental Family*, the story of a day-care center worker and a single dad with amnesia who find themselves falling for each other as she cares for their children together. And there's another CAVANAUGH JUSTICE offering in Special Edition from Marie Ferrarella: in *Cavanaugh's Woman*, an actress researching a film role needs a top cop— and Shaw Cavanaugh fits the bill nicely. *Hot August Nights* by Christine Flynn continues THE KENDRICKS OF CAMELOT miniseries, in which the reserved, poised Kendrick daughter finds her one-night stand with the town playboy coming back to haunt her in a big way. Janis Reams Hudson begins MEN OF CHEROKEE ROSE with *The Daddy Survey*, in which two little girls go all out to get their mother a new husband. And don't miss *One Perfect Man*, in which almost-new author Lynda Sandoval tells the story of a career-minded events planner who has never had time for romance until she gets roped into planning a party for the daughter of a devastatingly handsome single father. So enjoy the rising temperatures, all six of these wonderful romances…and don't forget to come back next month for six more, in Silhouette Special Edition.

Happy Reading!

Gail Chasan
Senior Editor

Please address questions and book requests to:
Silhouette Reader Service
U.S.: 3010 Walden Ave., P.O. Box 1325, Buffalo, NY 14269
Canadian: P.O. Box 609, Fort Erie, Ont. L2A 5X3

Joan Elliott Pickart

ACCIDENTAL FAMILY

Silhouette

SPECIAL EDITION

Published by Silhouette Books

America's Publisher of Contemporary Romance

For my daughters

SILHOUETTE BOOKS

ISBN 0-373-24616-1

ACCIDENTAL FAMILY

Visit Silhouette Books at www.eHarlequin.com

Printed in U.S.A.

Books by Joan Elliott Pickart

Silhouette Special Edition

*Friends, Lovers...and
  Babies! #1011
*The Father of Her Child #1025
†Texas Dawn #1100
†Texas Baby #1141
Wife Most Wanted #1160
The Rancher and the Amnesiac Bride #1204
∆The Irresistible Mr. Sinclair #1256
∆The Most Eligible M.D. #1262
Man...Mercenary...Monarch #1303
*To a MacAllister Born #1329
*Her Little Secret #1377
Single with Twins #1405
◊The Royal MacAllister #1477
◊Tall, Dark and Irresistible #1507
◊The Marrying MacAllister #1579
◊Accidental Family #1616

Silhouette Desire

*Angels and Elves #961
Apache Dream Bride #999
†Texas Moon #1051
†Texas Glory #1088
Just My Joe #1202
∆Taming Tall, Dark Brandon #1223
*Baby: MacAllister-Made #1326
*Plain Jane MacAllister #1462

Silhouette Books

*Her Secret Son
◊Party of Three
◊Crowned Hearts
  "A Wish and a Prince"

*The Baby Bet
†Family Men
∆The Bachelor Bet
◊The Baby Bet: MacAllister's Gifts

Previously published under the pseudonym Robin Elliott

Silhouette Special Edition

Rancher's Heaven #909
Mother at Heart #968

Silhouette Intimate Moments

Gauntlet Run #206

Silhouette Desire

Call It Love #213
To Have It All #237
Picture of Love #261
Pennies in the Fountain #275
Dawn's Gift #303
Brooke's Chance #323
Betting Man #344
Silver Sands #362
Lost and Found #384
Out of the Cold #440
Sophie's Attic #725
Not Just Another Perfect Wife #818
Haven's Call #859

JOAN ELLIOTT PICKART

is the author of over eighty-five novels. When she isn't writing, Joan enjoys reading, gardening and attending craft shows on the town square with her young daughter, Autumn. Joan has three all-grown-up daughters and three fantastic grandchildren. Joan and Autumn live in a charming small town in the high pine country of Arizona.

Dear Reader,

It is time to once again bid farewell to the MacAllister family. They came into my life and yours for the first time in 1995 with *Angels and Elves,* Forrest and Jillian's story, which introduced the ever-growing MacAllister clan.

Now, as we leave the MacAllisters to get on with their happy lives, Forrest and Jillian are grandparents, their triplet girls all having found true love.

I want to thank all of you who have written to me over the years to say you were enjoying the MacAllister series as well as my other books. I can't begin to tell you how much those letters mean to me.

Will the MacAllisters be back to visit you in the future? I really don't know. Only time will tell if they start whispering in my ear, urging me to share what has transpired as yet another generation grows into adulthood.

I hope you enjoy Patty and David's story as they deal with dark painful pasts that threaten to keep them from stepping into the sunshine of a future they might share together.

Thank you again for your continued support.

Warmest regards,

Joan Elliott Pickart

Chapter One

Patty Clark maneuvered her eight-year-old compact car through Ventura's heavy going-to-work traffic. It was a picture-perfect September day, and the glowing California sun in a brilliant blue sky dotted with puffy clouds promised to warm the chilly morning.

In the back seat, three-week-old Sophia slept peacefully in her secured carrier despite the fact that her three-year-old brother Tucker was chanting with the volume set on high.

"Sarah Ann, Sarah Ann, Sarah Ann," Tucker yelled happily. "I'm gonna see my bestis friend Sarah Ann. Right, Mommy? We gets to go to Fuzzy Bunny and I can play with Sarah Ann, Sarah Ann, Sarah Ann."

"Yes, that's right, Tucker," Patty said, laughing. "We're going to the day-care center today, but remember it's just this one time because Mommy doesn't work there anymore. They need my help because they don't have enough caregivers right now to take care of you busy bees.''

''And I gets to play with Sarah Ann,'' Tucker shouted.

''Hush, sweetheart,'' Patty said. ''You'll wake Sophia and she'll probably cry all the way to the Fuzzy Bunny. We don't want that to happen.'' She paused. ''Tucker, it's been a little more than three weeks since we went to the center every day. We don't know for certain that Sarah Ann still goes there. I don't want you to be disappointed if you can't play with her.''

''She'll be there,'' Tucker said, bouncing his hands on his booster seat. ''Her daddy bringed her all the time. Remember?''

''Yes, that's true,'' Patty said, ''but Sarah Ann started coming to the center only two weeks before we stopped going. Maybe her daddy doesn't bring her anymore.''

''Yes, he does,'' Tucker said, frowning. ''I know he does. Sarah Ann likes being at the Fuzzy Bunny and her daddy smiled at her 'cause she likes it. I'm going to play with Sarah Ann, Sarah Ann, Sarah Ann.''

Patty tuned out Tucker's excited mantra, realizing that her son was not going to accept the fact that his ''bestis friend'' might not be at the Fuzzy Bunny that morning.

Her daddy smiled at her.

Tucker's words echoed in Patty's mind as her thoughts drifted back to the two weeks that David

Montgomery had brought his daughter to the center before Patty had left to give birth to Sophia.

Oh, yes, she mused, the handsome-beyond-belief Mr. Montgomery had, indeed, smiled at his daughter before leaving her in the morning and when he picked her up at precisely 5:45 p.m. He did not, however, share that smile with any of the caregivers, nor take a moment to say the standard ''Have a nice day'' to the staff. His focus had been on Sarah Ann and that was that.

Except… Well, yes, there had been that very brief exchange between herself and David Montgomery on her last day at the center.

It had all started when Susan, one of the other caregivers who was delightful to work with, had rushed up to Patty before David Montgomery arrived with his daughter.

''Today is the day,'' the attractive Susan had said. ''I can feel it in my bones. This morning when David Montgomery delivers little Sarah Ann, he is going to smile at me. I've done everything but stand on my head to get that handsome hunk of a man to acknowledge my existence with more than a quick nod and a frown. But I have these vibes, Patty. I do. Today he will smile…at me.''

Patty had laughed. ''You're positive about that, Susan?''

''Yes, I am,'' she said, nodding decisively. ''We know he's a single daddy because there was no Mrs. Montgomery listed on the application blank he filled out for Sarah Ann. I am a single mommy. Therefore, it makes perfect sense that gorgeous David should get to know gorgeous me, which would go much more smoothly if the darn guy would smile at someone other than his daughter."

"Like you, for example," Patty said.

"Exactly," Susan said. "He's been bringing Sarah Ann here for two weeks now. Enough of this grumpy stuff." She paused. "Oh, there they are now, coming in the front door. This is it. Today is the day. Watch me in action."

Patty followed slowly behind Susan, deciding that if the determined Susan actually managed to get David Montgomery to smile at her it was worth witnessing. He was, indeed, an extremely good-looking man.

He was tall, had black hair like her own, wide shoulders, long, muscular legs that were outlined to perfection in the faded jeans he wore, and the most incredible blue eyes she had ever seen. It was no wonder that Susan was all a-twitter over the I-only-smile-at-my-daughter David Montgomery.

"Good morning, Sarah Ann," Susan said brightly, stopping in front of the pair. "And good morning to you, Mr. Montgomery." Susan beamed.

David Montgomery nodded, then turned his attention to Sarah Ann.

"Have fun, sweetheart," he said, smiling. "I'll see you later. I love you."

"Love you," the little girl said, then dashed off to join in the fun, her short black curls bouncing.

David's frown slid back into place as he watched Sarah Ann go without a backward glance at her daddy. Susan turned, rolled her eyes heavenward as she saw Patty standing there, then stomped off.

"Mr. Montgomery?" Patty said.

"Yes?" He switched his gaze slowly to Patty.

"I'm Patty Clark," she said. "This is my last day here and I just wanted to tell you how much I've enjoyed getting to know Sarah Ann. She's a bright, happy little girl."

"Thank you," David said, smiling. "I appreciate you saying that. I think she's very special, but I'd be the first to admit that I'm very prejudiced when it comes to my daughter. But please call me David and I'll call you Patty."

"All right, and I feel the same prejudiced way about my son," Patty said, laughing. "And I'm sure I'll do the same when this little girl arrives." She patted her stomach.

"You and your husband must be excited about having another child," David said.

"I'm...I'm not married," Patty said. "I'm divorced. But, yes, I'm certainly anticipating holding my daughter for the first time in just a few weeks. I..."

"Mommy," Tucker said, running to Patty's side.

"What can I do for you, sir?" Patty said, tousling Tucker's dark silky hair.

"Can Sarah Ann come to our house to play on another day?" Tucker said. "Sarah Ann is my bestis friend."

"We'll see, Tucker," Patty said. "But I can't promise."

"'Kay," he said, then ran off.

"So that's Tucker," David said. "Sarah Ann talks about him at home a great deal." He chuckled. "She says he's her bestis friend the same way Tucker said *bestis*."

"Picking your *bestis* friend is very important when you're three," Patty said. "Well, I must round up my group. Have a nice day, Mr. Montgomery...David. It was a pleasure chatting with you."

"I enjoyed talking with you, too, Patty," he said. "Goodbye."

As David turned and left the building moments later, Susan rushed to Patty's side.

"I don't believe it," Susan said, planting her hands on her hips. "He smiled at you, Patty. He even carried on an I'm-a-human-being conversation. That rotten so-and-so. What have you got that I don't?"

Patty laughed. "A fat stomach. I'm what you would call *safe*, Susan. Women who resemble beached whales are not generally known to be on the make, so to speak. You, my dear, are just too pretty. Hence, you're a potential nuisance to a man who no doubt has women fainting dead out at his handsome-beyond-belief feet.

"The fact that David Montgomery hasn't even smiled at anyone except me, the blimp, says he's focusing entirely on his daughter at this point in time. Get it?"

"I guess so," Susan said, scowling. "But I sure don't like it. What a sad waste of machismo." She smiled again. "Well, there's hope. The man can't stay grumpy forever, for crying out loud. Did you see that smile, Patty? It just lit up his face and..." Susan flapped one hand in front of her face. "I'm over-heating."

"Well, cool down and gather your wee ones," Patty said, laughing. "It's time to get organized here. With Marjorie at the dentist I'm in charge of this place for the moment and heaven forbid we don't stay on schedule. Shoo David Montgomery out of your mind.''

''Easier said than done,'' Susan said. ''Okay. I'm off to do my thing with nary a thought of hunky David. Today…ta-da…we finger-paint. Oh, ugh. I'm not in the mood for *that* mess.''

Patty splayed her hands on her lower back, then shifted her gaze to the door David had disappeared through.

There was a time long, long ago, she mused, when she would have daydreamed about a man like David Montgomery just as Susan was. But those days were over. Forever.

''Green light, green light, green light,'' Tucker yelled from the back seat, bringing Patty back to the present with a thud. ''Go, go, go.''

The driver of the car behind Patty honked the horn as though thoroughly agreeing with Tucker that Patty should get a move on. She pressed on the gas pedal while ignoring the warm flush on her cheeks.

That had been a ridiculous trip down memory lane, she thought with a mental shake of her head. Why she had relived that conversation with David Montgomery she didn't know. Well, enough of this nonsense.

Minutes later Patty was entering the Fuzzy Bunny, her arms full of Sophia in her carrier, her purse and a packed-to-the-brim diaper bag. Two caregivers waved from across the room. Tucker made a beeline for his favorite corner of the large sunny area where brightly colored, chunky wooden blocks waited to be turned into magical creations. Susan hurried to Patty and took the carrier containing a still-sleeping Sophia.

"Hello, pretty girl," Susan cooed at the baby, then shifted her attention to Patty. "Oh, cripe, look at you. You're skinny as a post already. Not a lump or a bump in those slacks you're wearing. How did you do that? Do you know that a woman asked me when my baby was due and I was standing there holding a newborn Theresa in my arms? Talk about depressing. Even worse is that was seven years ago and I still haven't shed the last ten pounds I gained during that pregnancy. Grim."

"You have a...lush figure, Susan," Patty said, smiling. "Very womanly."

"You'd make a good politician," Susan said, laughing. "Tell 'em what they want to hear."

"What I want to hear," Patty said, "is that David Montgomery is still bringing Sarah Ann here. Tucker is so excited about seeing his 'bestis friend' again and will no doubt pitch a royal fit if she doesn't show up."

"Oh, sexy David will be here with daughter in tow," Susan said, "and frown in place. The man has not smiled at anyone except his kiddo since he had that chitchat with you. Do you think it would help if I tore off my clothes when he arrives? No, forget that. The extra ten pounds I spoke of is not an inspiring sight to behold. Anyway, it's great to have you here today, Patty. Where do you want me to put Miss Sophia?"

"I'll use Marjorie's office for a nursery today since she's away on vacation. Sophia can camp out on the owner's turf."

"Okay, I'll carry her... Oops. Jeffery, the wheels stay on the truck. Do not... Too late. That kid kills a truck a day, I swear."

"Go play mechanic," Patty said, taking the carrier from Susan.

"Sarah Ann, Sarah Ann, Sarah Ann," Tucker yelled, racing across the room. "You came. I told my mommy you would."

Patty slid the heavy diaper bag and her purse onto one of the small child-size tables, then turned to see the front doors of the center swishing closed behind Sarah Ann and David Montgomery.

Oh, good grief, Patty thought. David Montgomery was even more ruggedly handsome than she remembered him being. He just oozed blatant masculinity, moved with a fluid male grace that said he was comfortable in his own body—a body that was so perfectly proportioned it was sinful.

Was that a sensual shiver slithering down her spine? No, it was not. Patty Sharpe Clark, don't be absurd.

In the next moment her eyes widened as Tucker and Sarah Ann threw their arms around each other in a hug. Patty hurried forward, aware that while the pair were the same age Tucker was a stocky little boy while Sarah Ann was small-boned and delicate. An exuberant hug from Tucker Clark could result in Sarah Ann being squished to tears.

"Tucker, honey," Patty said when she reached the children. "I know how happy you are to see Sarah Ann but you're going to squeeze the stuffing out of her. Let her go, Tucker."

"'Kay," Tucker said. "Are you still my bestis friend, Sarah Ann?"

Sarah Ann nodded. "You're my most bestis friend in the whole wide world, Tucker."

"Come play blocks," Tucker said, taking Sarah Ann's hand.

"'Kay."

"Goodbye, Sarah Ann," David said. "I love you."

"Love you," she said, not looking at him.

The dynamic duo ran toward the far corner of the room.

"Well," David said, chuckling, "I'd say that was quite a reunion." He shifted his gaze to Patty. "You've been busy since you were here last." He looked at Sophia, then back at Patty. "You have a beautiful daughter, Patty.

"I remember holding Sarah Ann when she was a newborn and thinking she was an honest-to-goodness miracle. I always thought I'd be the father to three or four kids, live in a home overflowing with love and laughter and…" He cleared his throat. "Does Tucker like his role of big brother?"

"He's not overly impressed," Patty said, laughing. "He wants Sophia to *do* something, not just eat and sleep."

"She'll get busy soon enough. They grow so fast. I've already been replaced as Sarah Ann's bestis friend."

"Oh, not really," Patty said. "Sarah Ann dashes off when she gets here because she's secure in the knowledge that you'll be back to get her later. You're her bestis daddy and she trusts you with such pure and awesome innocence."

"I hope I can live up to that trust," David said, looking directly at Patty.

"I...I'm sure you will," she said, meeting his intense gaze.

Those eyes, she thought, rather hazily. They put a Ventura summer sky to shame. So blue, so... Goodness, it was warm in here. There was a strange heat consuming her, churning and swirling and... David Montgomery was pinning her in place with those incredible blue eyes.

"Well, I'd better be on my way," David said, his voice sounding slightly strangled. "I assume you're reporting back to work here?"

"Oh, no, not really," Patty said, then drew a wobbly breath. "I'm just substituting today because they're short on caregivers."

"I see. Yes. Have a nice day. I'll be back to collect Sarah Ann at the usual time. Goodbye."

David spun around and strode toward the doors, soon disappearing from view.

"Goodbye," Patty said quietly, watching him go.

Sophia squeaked, stirred and opened her eyes.

"Hello, sleepy girl," Patty said. "Your silly mommy just got thrown off-kilter by a very handsome man, but there will be no more of that malarkey. I'm wearing my mommy hat and it's staying firmly in place."

Outside in the parking lot, David started the engine of his SUV, then hesitated before backing out, his gaze riveted on the door of the building.

Patty Clark was a very attractive woman, he thought. She appeared to be about thirty, had black, shiny hair that fell to just above her shoulders and dark, expressive eyes.

Even when she had been pregnant there was something about her that would definitely catch a man's appreciative eye. And now? Whew. He'd felt the heat coiling low in his body when he'd looked into the dark depths of her eyes.

Man, Patty had a rough road to go. Divorced, the mother of a busy little boy and a newborn daughter? Her husband must have been a real scumball to make taking on what Patty was facing seem a better choice than to stay married to the jerk.

The next time he felt overwhelmed by the single-parent role he'd think of Patty Clark and what she was dealing with. Pretty Patty. He hoped she had family to lend her a hand, both physically and emotionally, a support group. Even still, that wouldn't erase the fact that each night when Patty locked the door of her home against the world, she was alone to cope with the needs of those two children. Damn, that was a lot to handle and...

"Montgomery," David said, shaking his head. "Why are you sitting here like a dolt mentally minding someone else's business? Someone you don't even know, and will probably never see again after today?"

David put the vehicle in reverse, checked his mirror, then backed out of the parking place. But before he drove from the lot, he looked at the doors to the Fuzzy Bunny Day Care Center one more time, the image of pretty Patty Clark flickering in his mind's eye in crystal clarity.

* * *

It was a typical busy day at the Fuzzy Bunny. With twenty energy-filled children there were the usual squabbles, lots of laughter, a skinned knee that needed a special Bugs Bunny Band-Aid and a hug for the wounded warrior.

After lunch the children collapsed on tiny cots and took much-needed naps, allowing the caregivers to eat their own lunches and get a second breath. Patty ate quickly, then went into Marjorie's office to give Sophia a bottle. She settled onto the soft leather chair behind the desk and fed her hungry daughter.

Patty's mind drifted back to the conversation she'd had with David that morning.

He'd sounded so wistful when he'd spoken of having wanted a large family, she mused. Wistful and resigned to the fact that it wasn't going to happen. Where was Sarah Ann's mother, the woman who would have given David more children? David was probably wondering where in the world Tucker and Sophia's father was. But, of course, one did not ask such personal questions of a person one hardly knew.

Patty sighed.

Her tale of woe would sound like a badly written soap opera, yet it was her reality and she'd been dealing with it inch by emotional inch over the past months, gaining at least a modicum of inner peace.

But would she ever totally forget the devastating pain she'd gone through when Peter had moved out of their home and into his secretary's apartment the day after Thanksgiving, just before Patty had discovered she was pregnant with their second child? And as a Christmas gift? Peter Clark had served her with divorce papers one week before the special holiday.

She'd tried so hard to talk to him, to make him understand how sorry she was that she hadn't been an adequate wife, that she'd do much better in the future if he'd only give her another chance. But no, his mind was made up. Their marriage was over, he was in love with his secretary and that was that.

She had failed.

She'd done her very best to keep the house clean and picked up despite having a busy little boy who left a trail of toys everywhere. She'd prepared nourishing meals with Peter's favorite desserts made from scratch. She'd never pleaded fatigue or a headache when he reached for her in the night but... It hadn't been good enough. *She* hadn't been good enough.

She was a devoted mother. She knew that. But she had failed miserably in the role of wife to her husband, and because of that he'd left her for another woman who could and would meet his needs.

Because of her, Tucker rarely saw his father. More often than not he did not show up when he was scheduled to have Tucker for an outing. Tucker no longer asked about his daddy. When Peter did manage to come for his son, Tucker trudged out the doors with a frown on his little face, then ran into Patty's embrace upon his return.

And this new baby? Patty thought, gazing at Sophia. When she'd told Peter she was pregnant he'd rolled his eyes in disgust and told her to have her attorney contact his attorney about adjusting future child-support payments.

He never acknowledged her changing body when he came for Tucker, nor asked how she was feeling or if she knew if she was having a girl or a boy. He knew when the baby was due but he hadn't contacted her to see if she'd given birth. He just didn't care.

Because she had failed as a wife.

To Peter she was the mother of his children, nothing more. Because she had that title he was going to have to fork over a chunk of his paycheck every month to help feed and clothe those children. Patty was an ex-wife, and he'd moved on to be with someone who knew how to perform in that role properly.

"Patty?" Susan said, coming into the office and snapping her back from her tormented thoughts. "This is the first chance I've had to really speak to you alone. Has Peter seen Sophia yet?"

Patty shook her head. "He knew when my due date was, but I haven't heard from him. He hasn't shown up on his scheduled visitation days for several months to take Tucker for an outing, either. Tucker rarely mentions his daddy anymore. Well, it's Peter's loss. I have two wonderful children and I'm enjoying being a mother to them more than I could ever begin to express in words. Life is good."

"I don't know how you can be so cheerful," Susan said. "I'd have murder on my mind if a man did to me what Peter did to you, Patty. Every time I think about it my blood boils. But you? You just keep on smiling."

Because she'd cried until she'd had no more tears to shed, Patty thought.

Chapter Two

The afternoon passed quickly and just after five o'clock parents began to arrive to pick up their offspring before the center closed at six. At five minutes before six o'clock Susan planted her hands on her hips and stared at the front doors.

"That's strange," she said to Patty. "Ever since David Montgomery started bringing Sarah Ann here you could set your watch by him. He picks her up at five-forty-five on the dot, never, ever later than that."

"Well, ten minutes doesn't mean anything other than the traffic is heavier than usual," Patty said, sinking onto a rocking chair used for story hour. "You go ahead, Susan. I'll wait for David. Sarah Ann is the only child who hasn't been picked up and she and Tucker are playing nicely together with the blocks. Sophia just ate so she's fine, too. I'll use these few minutes to rest my weary self."

"I hate to leave you here alone," Susan said, frowning, "but Theresa's caregiver will be furious if I'm late."

"Then go, go, go," Patty said, flapping her hands at her. "I've worked here since January and no one has ever been later than a few minutes after six."

"Not during my two years here, either," Susan said. "I don't even know what Marjorie's policy is about it because it never came up. I wouldn't be concerned if it wasn't David Montgomery. He's just never late, Patty, and it's now six minutes after six. This is creepy. Something is wrong."

"It is strange that he hasn't phoned to say he's running late," Patty said. "You know, if he had a flat tire or something. He's devoted to Sarah Ann and... You're right. Something is wrong, but I don't have a clue as to what it is." She paused. "Well, I'll just sit here, relax and wait. Susan, go."

Susan glanced at her watch, cringed, then hurried toward the doors, disappearing from view moments later.

Patty shifted in the rocker to see that Tucker and Sarah Ann were still engrossed in their building project, then stared at the Mickey Mouse clock on the wall.

Something was *definitely* wrong, she thought, frowning. It was evident to everyone who worked there that David Montgomery's world centered on his daughter. For him to be late picking her up without a telephone call to explain his tardiness was totally out of character for him.

Dear heaven, it was nearly six-thirty. Where was

David? What had happened to him? What should she do?

David, please walk through that door. Now. Right now.

But David Montgomery did not appear and the clock kept ticking.

"Mommy," Tucker whined at six-forty-five. "I'm hungry."

"I know, sweetie," Patty said, getting to her feet. "Why don't you and Sarah Ann sit at one of the little tables and I'll get you some juice and crackers."

"My daddy?" Sarah Ann said, her bottom lip trembling. "I want my daddy."

"He'll be here, honey," Patty said. "Your daddy is just a bit late, that's all. Don't cry, Sarah Ann. Your daddy will come in a wink and a blink."

Now, David, she thought, staring at the doors again. *Forget the wink and blink and walk through that door.*

When Tucker and Sarah Ann were happily consuming their snack, Patty went into Marjorie's office and sank onto the chair behind the desk. The walls were clear glass and she could see the two children from where she sat. Sophia slept peacefully in her carrier on a loveseat set against the wall.

Think, Patty told herself. *Calm down and think. Okay. David had gotten a sudden case of the flu, was running a temperature and had fallen asleep at home because he was burning up with fever.*

She went to the filing cabinet in the corner and found the application David had filled out when enrolling Sarah Ann at the center. Moments later she punched in the number listed and the telephone rang on the other end. And rang and rang and rang. There was no other information on the form. No place of employment, no one to contact in an emergency. Nothing.

She replaced the receiver, sat down again and pressed her fingertips to her now-throbbing temples.

So much for that brilliant deduction, she thought. Now what? Hospitals. Oh, as grim as the idea was, maybe David had been in an accident and… Well, she'd start with the hospital she knew best. Mercy. Where Tucker and Sophia had been born.

The telephone book produced the number and Patty ignored her shaking hand as she pushed the buttons on the telephone. It was answered halfway through the second ring.

"Mercy Hospital. How may I direct your call?"

"I…um…I guess I should speak with someone in the emergency room, please," Patty said.

"One moment, please."

Two seconds of music played, then a new voice came on the line.

"Emergency."

"Yes," Patty said, wishing her voice was steadier. "I'm inquiring as to whether a David Montgomery has been brought into the emergency room there at Mercy Hospital."

"Are you a member of his immediate family?"

"Oh, well, I…" Patty said, her mind racing. "Yes. Yes, I am. I'm…I'm his wife. I'm out of town, you see, and phoned the house and David wasn't there, and I'm so worried and…"

"Let me check, Mrs. Montgomery."

More music echoed in Patty's ear and she drew a shuddering breath.

"Mrs. Montgomery?"

"Yes?"

"I'm sorry to tell you this, ma'am, but your husband has been in an automobile accident and was brought here to Mercy. We tried to contact next of kin and finally found your home number through the operator as a new listing, but no one answered the phone."

"I'm not there. I mean, I'm out of town as I said. Please tell me how David is."

"Mr. Montgomery is in surgery at the moment to set a broken leg."

"Oh, God," Patty whispered.

"He also sustained a blow to the head, has a concussion and we'll be monitoring him closely through the night for that. I know you want to get here as quickly as possible but please travel safely. We'll be waking him through the night because of his head injury but we fully expect him to be groggy. He really wouldn't know you are here."

"I understand," Patty said. "Thank you. Thank you very much for your time. Goodbye."

Patty dropped the receiver back into place and pressed her hands to her cheeks, feeling how cold her palms were against her flushed skin.

Go back to thinking, she ordered herself. What to do, what to do. Think. Okay. She was calming down. Gathering the facts. David was battered but alive. Mercy Hospital was the best in Ventura. But any wife worth the title would drive above the speed limit to sit by his side, whether he knew she was there or not.

But she wasn't David's wife, and when she'd been Peter's wife she hadn't been worthy of the title, so...so she was going to operate in the role she did best. Mother. David was receiving the best of care and she would see to it that his daughter did the same.

Patty left the office and went to the table where the children were sitting.

"I have a wonderful surprise for you two," she said, forcing a bright smile onto her face. "Sarah Ann is coming home with us, Tucker, and spending the night. Isn't that fun, Sarah Ann?"

"I want my daddy," the little girl said.

"Your daddy had a very important place he had to go tonight, honey," Patty said, "and you're going to have a wonderful time at our house. Tucker has toys to share with you and we'll eat dinner together and... Okay? Sure. Now let's get your snack stuff in the trash and off we go."

"This is great, Sarah Ann," Tucker said. "We'll have a play date and a sleepover. 'Kay?"

Sarah Ann nodded slowly. "'Kay."

Bless you, Tucker, Patty thought. *And David? Hear me, please, somehow, somehow, hear me. Don't worry about Sarah Ann because I'll tend to her as though she were my own. I swear I will. Just be all right, David. Please, please, please, just be all right.*

The next morning Patty sat at the large oak table in the huge sunny kitchen at her parents' home. Her mother, Hannah, sat opposite her daughter, a frown on her face as she listened to Patty's tale of David and Sarah Ann. Hannah Sharpe had the same coloring as Patty, with a few gray strands now visible in her dark hair.

"So, there you have it," Patty said. "I called the hospital this morning to tell David that Sarah Ann was with me, safe and sound, but the nurse on his floor said he was in X-ray. Since I'm pretending to be his wife I couldn't leave a message saying that Patty from the Fuzzy Bunny is tending to his daughter. So, I need to get to the hospital to put David's mind at ease. Thank you for watching Tucker, Sarah Ann and Sophia while I go."

"Oh, that's no problem," Hannah said. "Tucker and Sarah Ann are so cute together. With their dark hair they look enough alike to be brother and sister. And you know I adore getting my hands on Sophia Hannah."

"I really appreciate this," Patty said, getting to her feet. "Well, off I go. Good grief, I'm so nervous. How do you tell a man that you sort of kidnapped his daughter?"

"What you did was very caring, very thoughtful and loving," Hannah said, rising.

"I hope David views it that way, but it was the only solution I could come up with." Patty paused. "Where's Dad?"

"Playing golf with your Uncle Ryan. Neither one of them is a threat to Tiger Woods but they have a very good time. Off you go. You've already said goodbye to the kiddos so just be on your way. David Montgomery must be sick with worry this morning over what happened to Sarah Ann when he didn't arrive to pick her up last night."

"You're right. At least I can assure him that Sarah Ann is fine. But, oh, dear heaven, I am just so nervous."

At Mercy Hospital, Patty was directed to the third floor and given the room number for David Montgomery. She stood outside the closed door and smoothed the hem of her red top over the waistband of her jeans, acutely aware that her hands were not quite steady.

Get it together, she ordered herself. She was being so ridiculous. It wasn't as though she'd done an unforgivable thing by taking Sarah Ann home last night, and had to beg for David's forgiveness or... Oh, stop thinking, Patty.

She knocked on the door and heard a muffled directive to come in.

Forget it. She didn't want to come in, Patty thought. She was turning around and going home. She was... Darn it, enough of this nonsense.

She pushed the door open and entered the room.

"I...um...hello," she said, as the door hushed closed behind her.

David Montgomery was propped up against the pillows on the bed, a bandage at the hairline above his right eye. His right leg was in a cast from below the knee to the tips of his toes and suspended above the bed by a complicated-looking apparatus. He was pale despite his tawny skin. He was also staring at her with wide eyes and his mouth had dropped open a tad.

A short man in his fifties, wearing a white coat and standing next to the bed, smiled and approached Patty.

"I'm Dr. Floyd Hill," he said, his smile growing

even bigger. "I'm assuming you're Mrs. Montgomery, and I must say we are very glad to see you. This will solve a great many unanswered questions for us."

"Oh, no, I'm not Mrs. Montgomery," Patty said. "I'm not married to anyone. I'm Patty Clark and I have David's daughter Sarah Ann."

"I didn't marry you?" David said, shifting up on one elbow. "You gave birth to my child and I didn't marry you? What kind of bum am I?"

"Huh?" Patty said, totally confused.

"Oh, my head," David said, easing back onto the pillow and pressing the heels of his hands to his temples. "It's going to fall off and roll across the floor. Break it to me gently. Do you have any other kids I should know about?"

"Me? Well, yes," Patty said. "Tucker is three years old and Sophia is three weeks old. Of course, Sarah Ann is three years old, too. We're really into the number three at the moment."

"Ohhh," David moaned, closing his eyes. "I'm worse than a bum. I'm a sleazeball."

"Dr. Hill? David? Somebody?" Patty said. "Would you please explain what is going on here? I feel as though I've stepped into the 'Twilight Zone.'"

"Which is a rather accurate description of where your husband...excuse me...your...the father of your children is, himself, at the moment."

"The who?" Patty said, her eyes widening.

"David," the doctor said, "does the name Patty Clark ring any bells. Patty...Clark."

David opened his eyes and looked at Patty again.

"No," he said. "I have never heard that name, nor have I seen this woman before in my life."

"Huh?" Patty said. "Now wait just a minute here."

"David has retrograde amnesia from the blow he sustained to his head," Dr. Hill said. "He doesn't even remember his own name, which we were able to supply from credit cards and what have you in his wallet."

"You're kidding," Patty said. A funny little bubble of laughter that held the edge of hysteria escaped from her lips. "No, you're not kidding. How long is this amnesia thing going to last?"

"I have no idea," the doctor said, shrugging. "Every case is different."

"Well, isn't this just dandy?" Patty said, then marched to the bed and gripped the top bar of the rail. "David, read my lips. You...have...a...daughter... named...Sarah Ann. She...is...three. She...is...cute. She...misses...her...daddy. That...is...you."

"I don't know any Sarah Ann," David said, frowning. "She's only three and she misses me and... This is terrible. Well, it could be worse, I guess. At least she's with her mother. You. Patty."

"No, no, no," Patty said, shaking her head. "I'm not Sarah Ann's mother. You didn't list a name for her mother on the application blank."

"What did I apply for?" David said. "To be a sperm donor? Are you the mother of Tucker and Sophia?"

"Yes, but..."

"I apparently didn't marry Sarah Ann's mother,

but why didn't I marry you? This Sophia baby is only three weeks old? I must say you look sensational for someone who just gave birth. At least I know I have good taste in women. You're very pretty. Who do our children look like? You or me?''

"That's it," Patty said, throwing up her hands. "This isn't a conversation, this is a ridiculous stringing together of words that are totally insane. Dr. Hill, I can*not* talk to this man."

"Let's all just calm down and start over," Dr. Hill said. "Please, Miss…Ms…Patty, sit down, won't you?"

Patty sighed and sank heavily onto the chair next to the bed. The doctor pulled another chair over and sat next to her.

"Now then," Dr. Hill said, "perhaps you would be so kind as to explain to us what your relationship is with David, his daughter Sarah Ann and, of course, there's Tucker and Sophia."

"Yes, all right," Patty said, then looked directly at David. "But first I want to apologize for my behavior. I was just so stunned to discover you have amnesia that it threw me for a loop and I haven't been very patient with your misconceptions. This must be terrifying for you, David, to wake up in a hospital and not even know who you are. On top of that, you're obviously in pain. I'm sorry I was so rude."

"Well, I haven't exactly been a pleasant person, either," he said, meeting her gaze. "I suppose I should say something macho, such as, 'amnesia is no big deal and I'll just hang around until my memory jump-starts itself again.' But…but the truth of the matter is, you're right. This is terrifying, the most chilling experience I've ever been through. Thank you for understanding that, Patty.''

Patty nodded, then told herself with a very firm directive to stop gazing into the ocean-blue depths of David's eyes. Mesmerizing eyes. Eyes that held a flicker of pain and fear and made her want to reach out and take David's hand and assure him that everything was going to be fine, just fine.

But she couldn't move, she thought frantically. He was pinning her in place with those eyes. Her heart was doing a funny little two-step number and a strange heat was swirling within her, low and hot and...

Good grief, she thought, finally switching her attention to the water jug on the side table by the bed, this man was lethally sensuous.

"Excuse me?'' Dr. Hill said tentatively.

"What!'' David said.

He was having a heart attack, he thought. On top of his other physical woes, he was now having a full-blown heart attack caused by gazing far too long into the beautiful, dark eyes of Patty Clark. Heat was coiling low in his body and... He was being consumed by desire for a woman he didn't even know.

"Sorry,'' he said. "What was it you were saying, Dr. Hill?''

"Patty is going to share what she knows about you, David. This could be important information.''

"Yes. Yes, of course,'' David said. "You have the floor, Patty.''

"Well,'' she said, lifting her chin. "That application I referred to earlier is the one you filled out at the Fuzzy Bunny Day Care Center to enroll Sarah

Ann over a month ago. There was very little information on the form and you told the owner of the center that you'd get her the remainder of the data later."

"Mmm," Dr. Hill said, stroking his chin.

"All the caregivers at the center became immediately aware that you're devoted to Sarah Ann, David," Patty went on. "You didn't really interact, smile or anything with those of us who worked there, but when you looked at your daughter, spoke to her, the love for her just radiated from your eyes, from the expression on your face. You're a wonderful father."

"Imagine that," David said, his voice holding a hint of awe. He frowned in the next instant. "But I didn't write down anything about Sarah Ann's mother?"

"No. We assumed you were a single father who has custody of your daughter."

"That would be unusual," Dr. Hill said. "Perhaps you are a widower, David."

"My wife died?" David said. "Wouldn't I be aware of something that devastating?"

"There are no rules for amnesia," the doctor said. "It varies from person to person. Go on, Patty."

"You always pick Sarah Ann up at exactly five-forty-five," she said. "Yesterday I was helping out at the center because they were short on caregivers. I no longer work there since I had Sophia. Anyway, you didn't show up to get Sarah Ann last night, David."

"Oh, God, my daughter must have been scared out of her mind. I don't know what she looks like, or what kind of personality she has, but that has got to be a terrifying experience for any three-year-old. I've got to go get her and…''

"No, wait," Patty said, raising one hand. "I took Sarah Ann home with me. She and my son Tucker are 'bestis friends,' as they put it. I told Sarah Ann that you had somewhere important you had to go and made the whole sleepover seem like an exciting adventure. The three kids are at my mother's right now so I could come here. And for the record, you are not related to Tucker and Sophia. I'm divorced from their father. Oh, and Sarah Ann slept well and ate a big breakfast. She's doing fine.''

"Thank you," David said, then drew a shuddering breath. "Thank you so much for what you did for Sarah Ann." He paused. "You have a son? And a new baby? And you're alone, but you took on another child? My Sarah Ann?''

"Yes," Patty said, shrugging. "I mean, goodness, what would you have had me do? I realize I have a lot on my plate but I can handle three children.''

"Amazing," David said. "You're a remarkable woman, Patty, and a natural-born mother, that's for sure.''

Oh, yes, Patty thought. She got high scores for motherdom. Total zero for wifedom.

"Patty," Dr. Hill said, "how was David dressed when he brought Sarah Ann to the day-care center? Suit and tie? Professional attire?''

"No, he wore jeans and a shirt.''

"But he doesn't have calluses on his hands as a construction worker might," the doctor said. "All right, let's recap what we know. The driver's license in your wallet, David, was a temporary one, indicating you probably moved recently and applied for a license with your change of address. The fact that we got your telephone number from the new listings operator strengthens that fact. But where you moved from, we don't know.

"We can surmise that you relocated approximately a month or so ago because that's when you enrolled your daughter in day care. Did you move across town? From somewhere else in California? Or from the other end of the country?"

"Damned if I know," David said wearily.

"You left your previous employment," Dr. Hill went on, "as evidenced by the lack of information on the day-care application and you saying you'd provide the data later. You're either looking for work, or a position is being held for you somewhere here in Ventura."

"But wouldn't the company be attempting to find him?" Patty said.

"Not if he arrived in town early to get settled in," Dr. Hill said. "The address on your driver's license is for a very affluent part of town. Whatever you do is lucrative."

"Maybe I'm a hitman," David said, then his eyes began to drift closed.

"He's exhausted," Patty said. "I'd best be going."

David's eyes flew open. "No, wait. What about my daughter? What's going to happen to Sarah Ann?"

"She'll stay with me until you're released from the hospital," Patty said.

"I can't ask you to do that."

"Do you have a better idea?" Patty said. "You

have to trust me, David, know that I'll give Sarah Ann the very best of care. I'll keep her home with us rather than take her to the Fuzzy Bunny so she can play with Tucker. I'll tell her that you have a booboo and will see her as soon as you can. I repeat...do you have a better idea?''

''No,'' David said quietly. ''No, I don't. I have to get out of this place. I have responsibilities. A child, a home, maybe a job I'm supposed to report to. Ah, hell, I hate this. I can't live this way. Doc, fix me.''

Dr. Hill chuckled. ''Patience, patient. Amnesia takes its own sweet time. Besides, we're keeping that leg elevated for the next several days to be assured there's no infection brewing before we fit you with a walking cast. You're stuck in that bed for now, David.''

''And I'm tending to your daughter,'' Patty said, getting to her feet. ''Sarah Ann is going to need clothes, though. I'm a member of a huge extended family with oodles of kids. Someone surely has clothes to fit her.''

''No, that's not necessary,'' David said. ''The keys that were in my now-totaled vehicle are in the drawer there. Go to my house and get Sarah Ann what she needs.''

''I wouldn't be comfortable going into your home, David.''

''But maybe she has a favorite toy she'll suddenly realize isn't with her, or a blanket she usually sleeps with or something,'' David said. ''She needs her own things around her. She needs her father, too, but... Hell.''

''I agree with David,'' Dr. Hill said. ''Sarah Ann

is caught up in the adventure of being at your house at the moment, but from what you're saying she and David are very close. I think it would be best that she at least have clothes and toys that are familiar to her until she can be united with the person who is the center of her existence.''

"Well, all right," Patty said. "I'll go to the house and get her some things. I'll call you here tomorrow, David, and see how you're doing. Maybe I should have you talk to Sarah Ann on the phone."

"Good idea," Dr. Hill said. "She's too young to be allowed to visit here in the hospital, but hearing her father's voice might be reassuring." He glanced at his watch. "I have an appointment. David, take a nap. Patty, it was a real pleasure meeting you. David and Sarah Ann are very fortunate to have you in their lives during this crisis."

Dr. Hill hurried from the room.

A sudden and heavy silence fell over the room, and Patty became acutely and uncomfortably aware that she was alone with David Montgomery.

Not that David Montgomery *knew* that he was David Montgomery, per se, nor did he have a clue that he had made hearts go pitter-patter each morning when he'd brought Sarah Ann into the Fuzzy Bunny. Well, not *her* heart, of course, but Susan certainly worked herself into a dither when she saw him and...

"Patty?"

Patty jerked at the unexpected sound of David's deep, rumbly voice.

"Hmm? Yes? What?" she said.

"I just wanted to say how grateful I am that you're taking care of my daughter. There really aren't words to express my gratitude.'' David paused and frowned. ''I wish I knew what Sarah Ann looks like so I could picture her in my mind. And where is her mother? Maybe Sarah Ann is with me because it's my turn to have her according to a visitation schedule of a divorce.''

''Maybe,'' Patty said, nodding slowly.

''Do you think it would be appropriate to ask a three-year-old about her mother? You know, 'So, Sarah Ann, where's your mom, honey?'''

''Well, sure,'' Patty said. ''If the opportunity presented itself so it could be done smoothly without Sarah Ann feeling as though she's being grilled or something. I'll try to do that but I can't promise anything.''

''Fair enough,'' David said, then yawned. ''Excuse me. It's not the company. I'm just wiped out.''

''Dr. Hill said you should take a nap,'' Patty said. ''I'll be on my way.''

''The keys to the house are in that drawer there.''

''Oh, yes.'' Patty opened the drawer and removed a key chain. ''Vehicle, house,'' she said, looking at the keys. ''I remember your address so I'm all set.''

''They told me my SUV is totaled. Some guy ran a red light and smashed right into me. I don't remember anything about that. Hell, I don't remember anything about anything. Dr. Hill said I shouldn't try to force my memory to return, but it's so frustrating not to know…. Enough of my complaining.''

''Sometimes,'' Patty said softly, ''things happen in our lives that we wish we could remove from our memory bank because they're so painful and… I'm not saying I'd like to have total amnesia like you have. That must be so frightening, so awful. But I wouldn't mind erasing some events. You know, like chalk from a blackboard.''

''Your husband...ex-husband hurt you very much, didn't he?'' David said, looking directly at her.

''Well, that's another story,'' she said. ''The issue at the moment is that you're going to take a nap and I am off to collect the children, then go to your house to get your daughter some clothes and toys. I'm still not that comfortable about going into your home but... I'll speak with you soon, David.''

''Thank you again. Don't give another thought to going into the house. I'm trusting you with my daughter so I'm sure not going to worry about the material things in my house. You don't look like a hardened criminal who's going to rob me blind anyway.''

Patty smiled. ''No, I'm not. Well, goodbye for now.''

''Bye,'' David said, then watched as Patty crossed the room and disappeared from view.

He sighed and closed his eyes, hoping sleep would give him a break from the physical pain he was in and from the emotional distress of having no memory, no sense of who he was, or what kind of a man he was.

Patty said he was a wonderful father. That was nice to hear and he'd believe her because it felt good. But who and what was David Montgomery the man? And where was Sarah Ann's mother?

''Give it a rest,'' he mumbled, as sleep began to edge over his senses.

Man, he'd just given the keys to his house to a woman he didn't even know. Was that dumb? But, hell, that same woman had his child and… He trusted Patty Clark. Yeah, he did. He trusted her. But he had a feeling, he just somehow knew, that he didn't trust easily, was wary and edgy in that arena. Why?

"Don't…know," he said. "All I actually know is that Patty sure is pretty. Pretty…Patty."

David drifted off into blissful slumber.

Chapter Three

"**M**y goodness," Hannah Sharpe said, after Patty related what she had discovered about David's amnesia. "That is quite a story. It sounds more like a soap opera than something taking place in real life."

"I know," Patty said, then took a sip of lemonade as she once again sat across from her mother at the kitchen table. "But it's true, unfortunately, and there is no way to know how long it will be before David gets his memory back."

"That would be so frightening," Hannah said, frowning. "Imagine waking up in a hospital and not knowing who you are or... I'd be absolutely terrified."

"David admitted that he *is* terrified," Patty said, running one fingertip around the edge of the glass. "I thought that was very honest of him, very real. Anyway, Sarah Ann will just have to stay with me until David gets out of the hospital.''

"Oh, honey, two three-year-olds and a newborn baby is going to be a lot of work.''

"It won't be so hard, Mom. Tucker will have someone to play with instead of wanting me to entertain him all the time. He's going to miss going to the Fuzzy Bunny, so having Sarah Ann at the house could very well make things easier for me.''

"We'll see,'' Hannah said.

"All I can do is take this one day at time,'' Patty said. "Well, I'd better gather the gang and go to David's to get Sarah Ann some clothes and let her collect a favorite toy or blanket if she has one.''

"David can't remember anything about where Sarah Ann's mother is?'' Hannah said.

"David can't remember anything…period. We agreed that if the opportunity presents itself, I'm going to ask Sarah Ann about her mother.''

"Hi, Mommy,'' Tucker said, running into the kitchen. "Sarah Ann and me is watching *Blue's Clues*.''

"Sarah Ann and *I are* watching *Blue's Clues*,'' Patty said. "Tucker, has Sarah Ann ever said anything about where her mother is?''

"Yeah, 'cause I asked her and she said her mommy was in heaven and she doesn't think she saw her mom before she went to heaven but she isn't sure but that's okay 'cause she has her daddy. I told her I don't see my daddy too much so she said I can say hello to her daddy whenever I want to. Can I have a cookie, Grandma?''

"No more cookies, Tucker," Hannah said. "You'll spoil your lunch."

"'Kay," he said, then ran back out of the kitchen.

"Well," Hannah said, "that was easy enough. We now know that David is a widower and apparently has been for quite a while."

Patty nodded, then shook her head. "Did you hear what Tucker said? He's resorting to borrowing Sarah Ann's daddy because he doesn't see his own very much. How Peter can turn his back on his own son and... No, I'm not going to get started on that subject."

"Good," Hannah said. "Fussing, fuming and raising your stress level is not going to change Peter Clark's behavior." She paused. "I was going to suggest you leave the kids here while you go get Sarah Ann some clothes and what have you, but I suppose she needs to be there to pick her favorite things."

Patty nodded, then got to her feet. "Thanks for babysitting, Mom. I now have to convince Sarah Ann that staying longer at our house is super-duper. She and David are very close and I'm expecting Sarah Ann's happy bubble to burst and the tears to start at any minute. Do you realize that David doesn't even know what his daughter looks like? That is so grim. I feel so badly for him."

"Why don't I take a picture of Sarah Ann with my digital camera," Hannah said, "then print it out on the computer? I'll come over to your place tonight, give the kids baths and put them to bed, while you take the picture to David at the hospital."

"Oh, I can't ask you to..."

"I'm volunteering," Hannah said, rising. "It will

be fun. I have nothing planned because this is the night for your father to attend his monthly meeting of retired police officers with your Uncle Ryan.''

"Well, okay, thank you," Patty said. "I'll go get the kids and you can take Sarah Ann's picture. That really is a wonderful idea.''

Tucker wanted his picture taken if Sarah Ann was getting hers done. Hannah printed out one each for the children, then an extra of Sarah Ann for Patty to take to David.

"Is my daddy coming now?" Sarah Ann said. "I want to show my daddy my picture.''

"Sarah Ann," Patty said, "your daddy bumped his head and his leg and got boo-boos. He has to be where they fix boo-boos for a few days. You're going to stay with me and Tucker until his boo-boos are better. You and Tucker can color him nice pictures this afternoon and I'll take them to the place where they tend to boo-boos and—''

"My daddy is in the place with the doctors that give shots and stuff," Sarah Ann yelled, then burst into tears. "I want my daddy.''

"So much for the boo-boo bit," Patty said. "Why are they always smarter than you give them credit for? Sarah Ann, sweetie, hey, don't cry. Your daddy is going to be fine, I promise you.''

"We'll take care of you, Sarah Ann," Tucker said, patting the little girl on the back.

"Yes, we will," Patty said. "Thank you for helping, Tucker. Sarah Ann, we're going to your house now to get you some clothes. Do you have a favorite toy you'd like to bring to our house?''

Sarah Ann's tears stopped as quickly as they had started.

"Yes, yes, yes," she said, jumping up and down. "I want my bear. His name is Patches."

"Okay," Patty said brightly. "Then we're off. See you tonight, Mom, and thanks again."

"Do I get a hug goodbye?" Hannah said, bending down and opening her arms.

Tucker immediately rushed into his grandmother's arms. Sarah Ann hesitated, then followed, allowing Hannah to hug her. A short time later the three little ones were buckled up in the back seat of Patty's car headed toward the Montgomery house.

Patty knew the general area, as it was where her grandparents Margaret and Robert MacAllister lived in their majestic home. When she got closer, she pulled to the curb and consulted a map from the glove compartment. David lived two streets away from the senior MacAllisters, who considered the entire Sharpe family part of the huge MacAllister clan.

Within minutes she turned into the circular drive-way leading to a two-story white stucco home with a red tile roof and a beautifully landscaped front area that sloped down to the sidewalk.

"My new house," Sarah Ann shouted. "I see my new house right there."

Patty turned off the ignition, assisted the children from the car, then scooped up Sophia's carrier.

"Do you remember where you lived before you came to your new house, Sarah Ann?" Patty said, as they started toward the front door.

"Brisco," Sarah Ann said. "Tucker, want to play with my toys?"

"Yeah," Tucker said.

"Brisco?" Patty said, frowning.

"Brisco," Sarah Ann said, nodding. "There were lots of hills on the streets and stuff and it rained whole bunches."

Patty inserted the key into the lock on the front door, hesitated, then looked at Sarah Ann.

"Do you mean San Francisco?" Patty said.

Sarah Ann nodded. "Brisco."

"Agatha Christie, eat your heart out," Patty said smugly as they entered the house. "Oh, your new house is lovely, Sarah Ann, very nice."

Patty swept her gaze over the large foyer, the sweeping staircase leading to the second floor, then stepped forward to peek into the large living room that boasted gleaming oak furniture and sofa and chairs in shades of blue, gray and burgundy.

A massive flagstone fireplace was on the far wall and flanked by floor-to-ceiling oak shelves that were partially filled with books. Cartons sat by the bookcases waiting to be unpacked. Patty placed a sleeping Sophia's carrier on the sofa.

"Come see my toys, Tucker," Sarah Ann said, heading toward the stairs.

"One hand on the banister," Patty said, "and go very slowly. I'll be up in a few minutes. I just want to check the refrigerator and make certain nothing is about to spoil."

"'Kay," the pair said in unison.

Patty walked down a wide hallway toward the rear of the house where she assumed the kitchen was.

This was David's house, she mused, drinking in details as she went, that he was turning into a home

for him and Sarah Ann. Just the two of them, because
Sarah Ann's mother was in heaven.

Was David still brokenhearted over the loss of his
wife and didn't even know his world had been shattered because he couldn't remember anything? That
was a rather depressing thought.

Patty entered the huge, sunny kitchen and made her
way through a multitude of boxes to reach the refrigerator.

Well, she thought, looking around, the kitchen was
obviously not high on the list of rooms to be set to
rights. She would guess that David wasn't eager to
cook, maybe didn't even know how to do much more
than make a sandwich or heat up soup. He and Sarah
Ann must have been eating out a great deal since
moving to Ventura, or he was bringing in take-out
food.

"I'm getting to be a very good detective if I do
say so myself," Patty said aloud.

She gripped the handle to the refrigerator, then
stopped, looking around again.

Strange, she thought. It was as though she could
feel, sense, David's presence in this house that was
becoming a home. She could picture him here so easily with Sarah Ann trailing behind him, chattering at
her daddy.

It was a very large home for two people, yet it felt
right for David. He would stride through these rooms
on those long, muscular legs, his blatant masculinity
demanding space to move freely. He would come to
this refrigerator where she was now standing, intent
on finding something inside to satisfy his desire to...

A man like David Montgomery would have strong,

powerful desires in any arena into which he stepped, whether it be to quell the need for food or to reach for a woman, sweep her into his arms and...

A shiver coursed through Patty.

What on earth was the matter with her? she thought, feeling the warm flush on her cheeks. She'd gone off on some embarrassing sensual trip about David sweeping a woman... Okay, Patty, admit it. The image in her mind had been David sweeping *her* into his arms, which was ridiculous. She didn't entertain mental scenarios like that, for heaven's sake, about a man she didn't even really know or...

"Enough of this nonsense," she said, then yanked open the refrigerator door. "Mmm. Pickings are slim."

There was a bowl of grapes, several oranges and apples, a jug of orange juice, a carton of milk and ready-made individual containers of pudding, Jell-O and yogurt. Three eggs, a half a loaf of bread, a jar of strawberry jelly, and that was it. The freezer above held a large box of Popsicles.

"This is all for Sarah Ann, I think," Patty said aloud. "Nope, David is not into cooking."

Going on the assumption that David was going to be in the hospital for several more days, Patty checked the sell dates on the offerings in the refrigerator. She found plastic bags beneath the sink and packed the milk, orange juice and the small containers of desserts. That done, she headed back in the direction of the stairs, placing the bags by the front door.

She made her way up the stairs and when she reached the top level of the house she could hear

Tucker and Sarah Ann laughing farther down the hallway.

Don't get nosy, she told herself, as she passed several rooms on her way to the children. Well, one or two little peeks wouldn't do any harm. No. But then again she might spot something that would give a clue as to what David did for a living and... No.

Sarah Ann's room was large and sunny, a little girl's paradise. It had a pink-and-white canopy bed, white bookshelves full of toys and books and a white dresser. The carpet was lush and the same smoky blue-gray color that she'd seen in the living room and covering the stairs and hallways.

"Sarah Ann," Patty said, "do you have a suitcase, honey?"

"In the closet," she said.

"I'll pack some clothes for you while you get Patches the bear."

"'Kay."

Patty completed her chore in short order, then turned to see Sarah Ann hugging a faded teddy bear.

"Is that Patches?" Patty said.

Sarah Ann nodded. "He's my bestis toy. He gots a hole one time and my daddy fixed him really good. See?"

A strange warmth seemed to tiptoe around Patty's heart and a soft smile formed on her lips as she saw the repair job David had managed to accomplish on the precious bear. There was a strip of dark blue duct tape across Patches's tummy, and hearts had been drawn on the life-saving bandage.

"Oh, that's a fine job of making Patches all better," Patty said. "Your daddy is a very good doctor."

"He only doctors toys and my boo-boos," Sarah Ann said. "That's all, 'cause he's busy when he wears a tie and doing turny stuff."

"I'm hungry, Mommy," Tucker said.

"What?" Patty said. Turny stuff? "Oh, hungry. Well, we're leaving now and we'll have lunch the minute we get home. Pick up those toys you were playing with, kiddos, and we'll be on our way."

He wears a tie to do his turny stuff, Patty thought, narrowing her eyes. Turny stuff. Tie. Suit and tie because he's...

"Sarah Ann," Patty said, nearly shouting, "your father is an attorney."

Sarah Ann planted her little fists on her hips. "I just told you that. My daddy is a turny when he puts on his tie."

"Got it," Patty said. "Let's go, my sweets. I may be the next Columbo but I still have to cook the meals."

Just before seven o'clock that evening Patty peered through the open doorway of David's hospital room and saw that he was propped up in bed watching the television mounted high on the opposite wall.

Goodness, she thought, the man just didn't quit. Even beat up and bandaged and wearing a faded hospital gown, there was an earthy male sensuality emanating from David Montgomery. He wasn't quite so pale tonight, his tawny skin standing out in stark relief against the pristine white pillow.

There was no readable expression on David's face as he watched what she realized was national news. Maybe he had been able to become engrossed in what he was hearing, forget for a few minutes that he was a man without a memory. And she was about to break his peaceful bubble and tell him his wife was dead. Being a detective was not all it was cracked up to be.

"Hello?" Patty said from the doorway. "May I come in?"

"Patty," David said. "Hey. Yes, come in. I didn't expect to see you again today. This is a nice surprise."

Man, he was glad to see her, he thought. His breath had actually caught when he'd heard her voice, seen her standing there. Patty was so lovely, so fresh-air pretty and...and he was overreacting to this woman due to the fact that she was the only lifeline he had to his reality, the slender link to his identity because she had known him before he lost his memory and she was taking care of his daughter.

That was the reason he got all hot and bothered when he saw Patty Clark. He was hanging tight to that explanation because the alternative was to admit he was having an adolescent testosterone attack, which wasn't very flattering.

"Sit down," David said, gesturing toward the chair next to the bed. He pressed the button on the remote control and turned off the television. "How are you? How's Sarah Ann? My daughter. Daughter. How can a man have a three-year-old daughter and not even know what she looks like?"

"Don't upset yourself, David," Patty said, sitting down in the chair. "The fact that you have amnesia is not your fault." She paused. "Dr. Hill was asking me earlier today what I knew about you while you were listening so I'm assuming it's all right to tell you what I've discovered about you. You know, without breaking any rules regarding what is or isn't said to someone whose memory is temporarily gone."

"It had better be a temporary condition," David said, frowning.

"I'm sure it is. I brought you a picture of Sarah Ann. Here."

David hesitated, then with a visibly shaking hand he took the piece of glossy computer paper from Patty and stared at the image of the smiling little girl.

"Oh, look at her," he said, awe ringing in his voice. "She's beautiful."

Patty smiled. "Yes, she is. She has your coloring. See? Black hair, your blue eyes. She's very intelligent, full of energy and chatters like a magpie when the mood strikes. She's small-boned, delicate, but that doesn't keep her from wanting to play whatever the other kids are into. You can be very proud of her, David. She's a wonderful little girl."

"But…but I don't recognize her," he said, closing his eyes for a moment, then looking at the photograph again. "Damn it, I know she's my daughter only because you're telling me she is."

"Give it time," Patty said gently. "Oh, these are cards that Sarah Ann and Tucker drew for you after I told them you had boo-boos."

David smiled slightly as he examined the pictures drawn with crayon on bright construction paper.

"Thank you," he said. "Tell Sarah Ann and Tucker I really liked these, okay? I appreciate your coming all the way back over here tonight to bring me these things."

"No problem. My mother came to the house and is doing her grandmother thing with all three of the children." Patty drew a deep breath and let it out slowly. "David, there is something I have to tell you."

"What is it?"

"Sarah Ann told Tucker that her mother—what I mean is... Oh, David, I'm so sorry but your wife is dead. Sarah Ann said that her mother is in heaven and she doesn't remember seeing her before she went there. But she also said it was all right because she had her daddy."

"My wife...Sarah Ann's mother is dead?"

"Yes. I'm sorry."

David looked up at the ceiling for a long moment, then met Patty's gaze again.

"Why aren't I registering any emotions about that? God, I hate this. I'm an empty shell. I look at a picture of my daughter and think 'cute kid, but I've never seen her before.' My wife is dead, for God's sake, and I have no reaction beyond 'oh, well.'"

"David, stop beating yourself up," Patty said, leaning toward him. "You must remember that your lack of memory is not your doing."

"Yeah," he said, dragging a restless hand through his hair. He narrowed his eyes. "Sarah Ann said she doesn't remember seeing her mother? Wouldn't I have given my daughter a picture of her mother?"

"There were no framed photographs in Sarah Ann's bedroom at your house," Patty said. "I didn't think anything of it until now. It does seem strange that you wouldn't keep her image where Sarah Ann could see it, feel connected to it, to her mother. Sarah Ann isn't upset by that. Her emphasis is on you.''

"It still doesn't make sense," David said, his voice rising. "It's as though I'm trying to get Sarah Ann to forget her mother even existed. What does that say about me?"

"That you don't have all the facts yet," Patty said. "Don't stand in judgment of yourself until you know why you seem to be distancing Sarah Ann from the memory of her mother. As an attorney you should gather all the data before reaching a conclusion."

"An attorney? I'm a lawyer?" David said, raising his eyebrows.

"Yep. 'A turny,' to quote your daughter. Oh, and you lived in San Francisco before you moved to your new house here in Ventura."

"Well, thank you, *NYPD Blue*," he said, smiling slightly.

"I'm Columbo, sir."

"Oh, okay," he said, chuckling. "You need a rumpled raincoat." He paused and frowned. "This is nuts. I can remember television shows but I don't recognize a picture of my own daughter?"

"Dr. Hill said there are no rules about amnesia, remember?"

"He wasn't kidding," he said, shaking his head.

"Well, I'd best let you get some rest."

"No," David said quickly. "I mean, do you have to leave so soon? This has been a helluva day stuck in this bed, trying to deal with all this and... Can you stay a little longer?"

"Yes, if you want me to."

"Thank you." David paused and frowned. "Well,

we can't share things about each other because I'm a blank page. Tell me about you, Patty Clark. Why are you a single mother of two little kids?''

It's none of your business, Mr. Montgomery, Patty thought with a flash of anger that dissipated as quickly as it had come. David was asking her a very fair question considering the fact she was poking around in her Columbo mode finding out everything she could about *him*.

''It's not a unique story,'' she said. ''My ex-husband fell in love with another woman and that was that.'' A woman who could meet Peter's needs as she had failed to do. ''Peter…Peter hasn't bothered to see Sophia and rarely takes advantage of his visitation times with Tucker anymore. Sarah Ann was so sweet about that when Tucker told her. She said he could say hello to you whenever he wanted to because she had her daddy. She's a darling little girl.''

''Why did you marry that jerk?'' David said, frowning.

''Well, for heaven's sake,'' Patty said, laughing, ''what a silly question. We were in love, floating around on cloud nine like any other couple who plans to marry. The first years were terrific. I taught school, Peter was climbing the ladder in the insurance company where he worked, we bought a home, the whole nine yards.

''We agreed that I'd be a stay-at-home mother and I quit teaching when Tucker was born. It's heartbreaking for me to realize that I'll need to go back to teaching second semester and leave my children with caregivers but…

''David, this is not interesting. It's just another sad

tale of a marriage that didn't make it. I usually don't pour out my woes like this. I'm living in the present now and looking to the future. There's nothing to be gained by dwelling on what happened between me and Peter, except that I did learn something important about myself.''

"Like what?"

"Enough of this. I'm changing the subject. Oh, Sarah Ann did have a favorite toy that she brought back to my house from yours. It's a worse-for-wear teddy bear that—"

"Patches," David said, then sat bolt upward. He sank back against the pillow in the next instant, one hand clamped on the top of his head. "Oh, my aching head. Forget the head. Am I right? Is Sarah Ann's favorite toy a beat-up bear named Patches?"

"Yes," Patty said, her eyes dancing with excitement. "Yes, you're right. Oh, David, see? Your memory is coming back in little bits and pieces. Do you remember anything else about Patches? You mended him with... Do you know?"

David stared into space. "No, there's nothing else there.''

"Don't worry about it.''

"What did I mend the bear with?"

"Duct tape," Patty said, smiling. "Then you drew hearts on it. I was very touched when I saw it. You really are a very loving father."

"I wonder what kind of husband I was?" he said, frowning.

No doubt a much better husband than she had been in her role of wife, Patty thought. She hoped when David's memory returned that would prove to be true, so he wouldn't have to live with the kind of guilt that tormented her.

"What's wrong?" David said. "You look very sad all of a sudden."

"It was just a fleeting thought, but it's gone now."

"You deserve to be happy, Patty."

"Oh?" she said, smiling. "You believe that, of course, because you've known me so well for so long."

"Laugh if you like," David said, looking directly into her eyes, "but while I don't even know at the moment how I like my eggs cooked, I do know that you are a very special, very rare and wonderful person who deserves to be happy."

"I'm happy," Patty said softly. "I have two children, two miracles, and I cherish my role as their mother."

"But what about Patty the woman? Is *she* happy?"

"I don't separate the titles, David. Patty the woman is a mother and I am happy."

"Mmm."

"What does that mean, that 'mmm'?"

"That even an empty-minded moron-at-the-moment like me knows that isn't how it's supposed to be," David said decisively. "Nope. Now, according to what I've been told I'm a father and I'm an attorney. However, I am also a man who, when I can remember what they are, has wants, needs, desires as do you, Patty the woman."

"Wrong."

"No, I'm not," David said, with a burst of laughter. "And I'm beginning to have no difficulty believing that I'm an attorney because I'm obnoxiously sure of myself when I take a stand.''

''That's for certain,'' Patty said, smiling.

''Ah, Patty, thank you,'' David said. ''You actually made me laugh right out loud and the way I've felt all day I wondered if I'd ever do that again. I owe you so much for so many things, the most important of which is your willingness to take care of Sarah Ann until I can get out of this place.''

''No more thanks are necessary, David.''

''Well, I do want to say that I'm very glad that you came into my life when you did, Patty Clark. Very, *very* glad.''

Chapter Four

Just before dawn the next morning, Patty crawled back into bed after feeding Sophia. She wiggled into a comfortable position, closed her eyes and waited for sleep to come, knowing she needed all she could get to provide energy for the busy day ahead.

But just as they had after she'd returned from the hospital the previous night, David's words spoken in a voice ringing with sincerity echoed in her mind.

I'm very glad that you came into my life when you did, Patty Clark. Very, very glad.

Oh, drat, she fumed, why was she being haunted by that statement? It was very clear what David meant when he said it. She was caring for his daughter during a stressful crisis in his life. Also, because of his amnesia, she was the only person he felt a link to, someone he sort of knew, and that helped his anxiety a tad considering he didn't even recognize Sarah Ann from her picture. So, yes, at the moment, David Montgomery was glad that Patty had come into his life. It was very simple really.

But...

She couldn't forget the warmth that had suffused her when David said what he'd said. She'd felt special and important and...and womanly. The very essence of her femininity had seemed to come alive, emerge from the dusty corner where she'd pushed it after Peter had left her. A virile, masculinity-personified man was very glad she had come into his life and...

"No," she said, pressing her palms to her temples. "Just stop it right now."

She wasn't *in David's life* in that context, not even close, nor would she want to be. No. She was finished with man-and-woman relationships, with having to once again face her inadequacies in that arena.

She was staying where she belonged, where she excelled, in the role of mother, and that was what David had meant by what he had said.

"Have you got that yet?" Patty said. "Go back to sleep while you can and knock off the nonsense, Patty Sharpe Clark."

But sleep wouldn't come and she finally left the bed when she heard Tucker and Sarah Ann giggling down the hall. Her day had officially begun.

In the middle of the afternoon, after naps, including one taken by Patty, she asked Sarah Ann if she would like to talk to her daddy on the telephone.

"No," Sarah Ann said, folding her little arms over her chest. "I want to go get my daddy right now."

"I know you do, sweetie," Patty said, "but he can't leave the hospital yet because of his boo-boos. Wouldn't it be nice to say hello to him, though?"

"Guess so," Sarah Ann said, nodding. "'Kay."

"I want to talk to him, too," Tucker said.

"Well, we'll see," Patty said.

A few minutes later, David answered the telephone in his hospital room.

"Hello?"

"David? It's Patty. I have a lovely little girl here who would like to say hello to her daddy."

"Really? Oh, geez, wait a minute, Patty. What do I say to her? I don't know how I chat with her. Have you ever heard me call her a nickname that she'll be expecting to hear? Like princess? Or pumpkin? Or whatever?"

"No."

"What do I say?"

"Yes, you're right," Patty said, glancing at Sarah Ann, "that *was* a pretty picture she colored for you and I'm sure she'll be pleased to know you liked it."

"I drew a picture, too," Tucker said.

"I heard that," David said. "Okay. The pictures. What else?"

"She's standing here waiting for the phone, David," Patty said.

"Oh. You can't help me out anymore because she'll hear you."

"That's how it is."

"I'm a nervous wreck."

"Handing over the phone now," Patty said.

Sarah Ann clutched the receiver with both hands. "Hi, Daddy...I miss you, too...I want you to come home now. Right now… No. I don't want to wait… No, no, no.'' She burst into tears and dropped the receiver.

Patty snatched it up. "David?"

"I blew it. Oh, man, listen to her. Her heart is breaking, Patty."

"Hold on a minute," Patty said, then placed the receiver on the kitchen counter. "Popsicles? Outside?"

"Yes, yes," Sarah Ann and Tucker said in unison.

"I want to hear a thank-you," Patty said, producing the treats.

"Thank you," the pair echoed, then dashed out the back door.

Patty picked up the receiver again. "End of crisis. When in doubt, bribe 'em."

"Sarah Ann stopped crying that fast?"

"Turned off the tears like a faucet," Patty said, laughing. "Well, lesson learned. Hearing your voice is upsetting to her when she can't see you. We won't do that again."

"One broken heart mended by a Popsicle," David said. "Amazing. Too bad that doesn't work for adults, huh? You sure read her like a book, Patty."

"I've had practice at this sort of thing, David." Patty paused. "How are you feeling today?"

"Not bad, except for that fact that I'm going out of my mind being trapped in this bed. I'm going to pressure the doctor when he shows up to spring me from this place."

"And how do you intend to care for your daughter?"

"Well, I... Hell, I don't know," David said. "I'll hire a housekeeper or something."

"And tell that woman what?" Patty said. "What time does Sarah Ann go to bed? What does she like to eat? What rituals and routines do the two of you have? Do you realize how devastating it would be to her if you forgot something that is very special and important to the two of you? She'd be hurt and confused, think you forgot about her because you were away for a few days."

"Well, what in the hell am I going to do?" David said, none too quietly.

"There's only one solution to this," Patty said. "You'll stay here at my house with Sarah Ann until you get your memory back."

What? she thought in a flash of panic in the next instant. What?

"What?" David said.

"I'm thinking as a mother, David, and putting Sarah Ann's needs before yours. I'm sure you'd be more comfortable in your large home, but can you understand how difficult that would be while you have no memory of Sarah Ann's routine and such?"

"Yes, but Patty, you don't even know me. How can you even entertain the idea of taking a stranger into your home? Oh, man, what a complicated mess this is."

"I admittedly don't know you, the man, that well," Patty said, "but I do know you, the father. That's what I'm basing this plan on." She paused. "Uh-oh, Sophia is awake and not too happy about something. I've got to go. Think about what I've proposed and we'll discuss it in more detail later. 'Bye."

"Goodbye," David said, then realized he was speaking to the dial tone.

He replaced the receiver, sank back against the pillow and stared at the ceiling.

This was nuts, he thought. Move into Patty's home when he left the hospital? Crazy. He apparently had a large house waiting for his return and that was where he would take his daughter. The two of them would be just fine.

Sarah Ann could go to day care and… Oh, really? And just how did he propose to get her there? Put her in a taxi? He couldn't drive with a cumbersome cast on his leg. Hell, he didn't even have a vehicle at this point because his was smashed to smithereens.

Okay, back up here. He'd call an agency and ask them to send applicants for the position of housekeeper with the stipulation that the woman would take Sarah Ann to and from the day-care center.

But Sarah Ann would need breakfast first, of course, and he didn't have a clue what his own child liked to eat. Nor what time she went to bed, or if she liked bubbles in her bath, or a story read to her as she snuggled beneath the blankets on her bed.

David reached over to the table next to the bed and picked up the picture of Sarah Ann.

"Oh, little girl," he said, staring at the photograph, "you are so pretty, so innocent, and you trust me to take care of you."

He couldn't bear the thought of his daughter looking up at him with confusion and hurt radiating from those big blue eyes when she realized her daddy didn't remember what they shared together. There was no way to explain amnesia to a three-year-old. *I don't exactly know who you are at the moment, kiddo, but I'll get back to you on that.*

But move into Patty's home?

As out of left field as the idea had struck him, it was beginning to make sense. If Patty had to ask Sarah Ann what her likes and dislikes were, it would seem very reasonable. He could listen and learn while waiting for his memory to return.

It wasn't as though, as Patty had said, she was inviting David Montgomery, a man she hardly knew, to reside under her roof. No. She was viewing him in his role of father, nothing more, doing what she believed was best for his daughter.

Did...well, did Patty Clark *ever* look at him through the eyes of a woman weighing and measuring his merits as a man? Ever? He had a feeling she didn't, which for some unknown reason was rather depressing.

He'd certainly scrutinized Patty as a woman, shame on him. Not just a mother. A woman. And he'd come to the conclusion she was very fresh-air pretty, so lovely. He really liked the way her dark, silky hair swung when she moved her head and those dark eyes of hers? Whew. Those eyes. Imagine them when she was consumed with sensual desire, wanting, needing, what a man, what *he* would bring to her and...

"Whoa, Montgomery," he said aloud, as heat rocketed through his body. "Don't go there. As far as Patty Clark is concerned you're a father, not a man, per se. End of story."

A man, David mused. A man whose wife had died long enough ago that Sarah Ann didn't recall whether she had ever seen her mother. When his wayward memory finally decided to come back where it belonged, would he discover that his heart was shattered over the loss of his wife, his life's partner, his soul mate?

Would he realize that he was so consumed with grief that he couldn't fathom ever loving again? God, how could a man not know if he was an empty shell because he had lost the woman his world revolved around?

Stop, he told himself. He would drive himself over the edge trying to reach for emotions that just weren't there yet for him to own.

He needed to concentrate on Patty's plan, be prepared to give her an answer the next time they spoke. He should do a pro and con thing about the idea of moving into her house. The problem with that was he couldn't think of a single reason why going to his own house would be better and make more sense. Doing that could very well break his daughter's heart when he didn't perform as the daddy she knew and loved.

So? Bottom line? He really had no choice but to take Patty up on her generous offer. He'd move into her house as Sarah Ann's father, not as a man, nope, no way, only as a daddy. He'd live under the same roof with pretty, pretty Patty.

"Take a nap," David said. "You just wore out your brain."

After ending the telephone conversation with David, Patty looked out the back door and saw that Tucker and Sarah Ann were sitting on the glider on the swing set, enjoying their Popsicles.

She rushed down the hall to Sophia's room, the nursery that was decorated in pale yellow and mint green. She scooped up the wailing baby, changed her very wet diaper, then sat down in the rocking chair and moved it gently back and forth.

It was becoming very clear, Patty thought, smiling at the baby, that Ms. Sophia Hannah did not like to be clad in a soggy diaper. Only three weeks old and her personality, likes and dislikes, were taking shape. She knew who she was and what was acceptable in her little world.

Oh, how difficult it must be for a grown man not to know what everyone, even three-week-old babies, took for granted. David Montgomery didn't know who he was, what made him happy, sad, contented or edgy. Nor did he have a clue as to what he shared with his precious Sarah Ann.

She'd shocked herself nearly speechless when she'd told David he should move into this house until his memory returned. But now that a little time had passed it made perfect sense. It was the only answer to the dilemma.

And it wasn't as though she was opening her door to a man she barely knew. No. She was very secure in the knowledge that David was a devoted and loving father, had seen him perform that role at the Fuzzy Bunny. It was David the father who would be coming here.

It was of no importance whatsoever that David happened to be the most incredibly handsome male specimen ever to cross her path. Immaterial. And the few little shivers and funny tap-dancing heart numbers she'd experienced while in close proximity to him? No big deal. Nope. Not worth dwelling on.

It would simplify things if David didn't have those mesmerizing blue eyes. Eyes like the blue ocean that a woman could drown in, just blank her mind and allow herself to succumb to…

"Sophia," Patty said, gazing at the baby in her arms, "write this down. I, Patty Clark, am a mother, not a woman. David Montgomery is a father, not a man. I'd like that in triplicate, please, and I'll sign all copies. Oh, you poor little thing. Your mother is a cuckoo."

That evening Dr. Hill sat by David's bed and nodded.

"Works for me," the doctor said. "There's no sign of infection in your leg, the scrape on your head is healing nicely. Tomorrow morning we can change out of that cast to a lighter one, but you'll have to use crutches and keep your weight off that leg until I give you the go-ahead to clomp around on it.

"Since you're leaving here to go where you can spend the majority of your time off your feet entirely, have meals prepared for you, what have you, I have no problem with releasing you tomorrow. You either stay in bed, or if you're up, your leg should be propped on something to keep it straight out, level. Got that?"

"Yeah," David said gruffly. "What I 'don't got' is a memory, doc. I'm not a happy camper."

"Do you like chocolate ice cream?" Dr. Hill said.

"Only with chocolate sauce on it." David's eyes

widened. "Hey, I remembered how I like my chocolate ice cream."

"You actually don't know just how much you *do* remember at this point," the doctor said, "because you've been staring at the four walls in this room. Being with your daughter may trigger a great number of things. You might get your memory back in bits and pieces, or all at once because something pushed the right button. Just stay calm and let it come naturally. That picture of your Sarah Ann is great, by the way. What a cute kid. What's her favorite television show?"

"*Blue's Clues,*" David said, with no hesitation.

Dr. Hill chuckled and got to his feet. "I don't think you'll be bunking in with Good Samaritan Patty Clark for very long, David. Your memory is hovering just below the surface where you can't quite get a handle on it, but it's on its way back. Trust me. I'll go write the orders for the changing of your cast and the okay to release you and blah, blah, blah. Have a good night."

"Thanks, doc," David said, then reached for the receiver on the telephone.

"You two settle down in here," Patty said, standing in the doorway of Tucker's bedroom. "You should both be asleep by now and I don't want to hear another peep."

"'Kay," Tucker said.

"'Kay," Sarah Ann said, from where she was snuggled on the lower part of Tucker's trundle bed.

"I mean it," Patty said. "I love you, sleep tight,

don't let the bed bugs bite, and I'll see you in the morning.''

Feet up now, Patty thought, starting toward the living room and allowing herself an audible weary sigh.

Sophia began to wail.

''Ohhh, darn,'' Patty said, stopping her trek. She listened for a moment. ''Hungry. That cry means hungry. Okay. Feet up will just have to wait a bit until I—''

The telephone rang.

''I don't believe this,'' she said, rushing into the kitchen and snatching up the receiver of the wall phone. ''Hello?''

''It's David. You sound…hassled.''

''Just a tad,'' Patty said, her shoulders slumping. ''I need to feed Sophia, David.''

''Oh. Well, I'll make this quick then. I talked to the doctor and explained your idea, and he said that as long as I stay off my feet and…''

''David, I don't mean to be rude, but could you cut to the chase?''

''Right. I'm taking you up on your generous offer to allow me to stay there at your house for a short time. For Sarah Ann's sake, you understand. If you could go by my house and bring me some clothes— mine were demolished in the emergency room—I can get out of here tomorrow and come…live with you.''

''Oh. Well. Sure. That's good. The best thing for Sarah Ann. Yes, it certainly is. Okay. Fine. Tomorrow then. 'Bye.''

Patty slammed the receiver back into place, then pressed her hands to her cheeks.

''Oh, my stars,'' she whispered. ''What have I done?''

Chapter Five

"**Y**ou've done *what?*"

Ted Sharpe, Patty's father, lunged to his feet, planted his hands on the kitchen table in the Sharpe home and frowned at his daughter as he leaned toward her.

"I...I invited David Montgomery to stay at my house until his memory returns," Patty said, wishing her voice was a tad steadier. "It's the best thing for Sarah Ann, Dad. It would be terribly upsetting to her if she learned that her father doesn't remember her, but with this plan she won't ever know."

"And you don't know diddly about this guy," Ted said, none too quietly.

"David is a devoted father," she said, lifting her chin.

"So are members of the mob," her father said. "No. I won't allow this, Patricia. Absolutely not."

"Honey," Hannah said, "Patty is a grown woman capable of making her own decisions."

"Oh, really?" Ted said. "What's next? She *decides* to become pen pals with Charles Manson?"

"Now that," Hannah said, laughing, "is funny."

"This is not a laughing matter, Hannah," Ted said, sinking back onto his chair. "This man is going to be living under the same roof with our daughter and grandchildren."

"Dad, listen to me," Patty said. "You're getting into your cop mode and that's not fair. The focus here is on Sarah Ann. I trust my instincts as a mother and this is the best plan. Besides, David can barely get around because he has a broken leg and will be using crutches. That will really slow him down if he decides to murder all of us in our beds."

"Patty, you are pushing me," Ted said, narrowing his eyes. "You and your mother seem to think there is nothing to be concerned about here. Well, fine, just chuckle your little hearts out, but I intend to use my connections and run a background check on this Montgomery jerk. And another thing. How do you know this amnesia bit is real? He could be a con artist who uses that ploy to…"

"Oh, spare me," Patty said, getting to her feet. "Dad, I know you're upset because you love me and the kids, but there is nothing to worry about. I went to David's house before coming here, a very nice home over by grandma and grandpa's, by the way, packed some clothes for him—"

"You messed around in his underwear drawer?" Ted roared.

"Oh, for heaven's sake," Hannah said, laughing

again. "Ted, would you calm down? Tucker and Sarah Ann are going to hear you bellowing."

"I've got to go," Patty said, getting to her feet. "I talked to David on the phone this morning and I don't want to be later arriving to pick him up than I said I would be. I'll get him settled in at the house, then come back for the kids. Thanks for babysitting, Mom."

"You're welcome, sweetie," Hannah said.

"I'll see you this evening, Patricia," Ted said, folding his arms over his chest. "In fact, I just might bring your Uncle Ryan along when we come to call. Two cops are always better than one."

"Don't you dare grill David as though he was under a bare light bulb," Patty said, planting her hands on her hips. "Or do a good-cop, bad-cop routine on him with Uncle Ryan. I'd be absolutely mortified."

"Would I embarrass my darling baby girl?" Ted said, an expression of pure innocence on his face. "Don't be silly."

"Mother," Patty said, "can't you control your husband?"

Hannah smiled. "We're back to really funny again."

"Goodbye, Mother, and the man you're married to," Patty said, spinning around. "I'll be back as soon as possible to get the kids."

"What did we do wrong raising her?" Ted said, as Patty disappeared from view.

"Nothing," Hannah said. "I think this is marvelous. Oh, Ted, it's been months since we've seen that kind of spunk and determination in our daughter. She's been so...so beaten down by the emotional upheaval of what Peter did. The Patty who just left here is vibrant, alive and her eyes were actually sparkling.''

"I realize that," Ted said, "but it does not erase the fact that David Montgomery is a total stranger and... I'm going to go call Ryan.''

As Ted strode out of the room, Hannah looked in the direction her daughter had gone, a soft, womanly smile on her face.

"This is your room, David," Patty said, sweeping one arm through the air. "As you can see, it has a king-size bed and the bathroom is right there, and I think...hope you'll be comfortable here.''

"This is the master bedroom," David said, frowning. "Where will you sleep?"

"There's a daybed in Sophia's room. I'll be fine in there.''

David moved forward with jerky steps as he struggled with the crutches, then sank onto the side of the bed.

"I can't put you out of your own bed," he said.

"Well, I don't happen to have a zillion bedrooms like you do at your house," Patty said. "I realize this home is much smaller than you're used to but—"

"Patty, I have no idea what my house looks like."

"Oh. Right. Sorry. Look, we'll make the best of it, okay? Just focus on Sarah Ann, David. We're doing this for her.''

David sighed, then nodded.

"Man, I feel like I walked all the way here from the hospital," he said. "Dr. Hill said it would be a while before my energy came back after suffering such a severe physical trauma. This is just dandy. No zip. No memory. Hell.''

"Quit feeling sorry for yourself." Patty paused. "I hope those aren't your favorite jeans that I slit the leg on to go over your cast."

"I have no idea," he said, glancing down at the faded material.

"Never mind. I'm going to go get the kids now. You stretch out on the bed and rest while I'm gone. You're going to need all the energy you can muster because I have a feeling that Sarah Ann is going to stick to you like glue once she sees you. I'm off. I'll fix us all some lunch when I get back."

"Wouldn't it be easier to get take-out delivered?" David said. "There's money in my wallet to pay for it."

"Maybe we'll do that tonight, get a pizza delivered. I have plenty of fixings for sandwiches for lunch."

"But I feel like I'm turning you into a maid, or a waitress, or—"

"I'm a mother, David. I'm certainly capable of preparing nourishing meals. Now stop fretting about everything and relax while I'm gone. Would you like me to turn the bed down for you?"

"No, thank you."

"I'll be back soon. Rest. Now."

Patty hurried from the room and David frowned as he watched her go.

"Yes…Mother," he said gruffly, when he was certain Patty couldn't hear him. "I know I should be grateful, but I am really hating this. I feel like the third three-year-old under Patty's care, for Pete's sake.''

After less than graceful maneuvering, David managed to stretch out on top of the spread. He turned his head to look at the empty expanse of bed next to him.

Patty sleeps here, he thought. He was in, on—whatever—Patty's bed. Did she sleep on her back, or her stomach, or maybe curled up on her side? That silky hair of hers would fan out over the pillow just beckoning willing fingers to sift through it. Her lips might be slightly parted in slumber, inviting a kiss, then a tongue to slip into the dark sweetness of her mouth and...

''Whoa,'' David said, as his body reacted to his sensuous mental wanderings.

He yawned, blinked several times, then drifted off to sleep.

David emerged slowly from a deep sleep and registered rather foggily the fact that a very heavy fly was sitting on the end of his nose. He opened his eyes, turned his head and found himself staring at eyes the same color as his that were only inches away. The fly on his nose was one small finger that was now removed.

''Hi, Daddy,'' Sarah Ann said, smiling. ''Patty said I could wake you up for lunch if I didn't bump your boo-boo.''

''I... Hello, Sarah Ann,'' David said, his voice rough with sleep. ''It's really great to see you.''

''I missed you whole bunches, Daddy,'' she said, her bottom lip beginning to tremble. ''I really did.''

"Oh, don't cry. I'm here now and I'm going to be just fine. I missed you, too. Why don't you go tell Patty that I'll be out in a minute."

"'Kay," Sarah Ann said, then ran from the room.

David dragged both hands down his face, carefully avoiding the still sensitive scrape high on his forehead.

That beautiful child, he thought incredulously, was his daughter. She was even prettier than she had been in the picture Patty had brought him. She was tiny, small-boned, but obviously full of energy. And she'd missed him whole bunches, which made him feel about ten feet tall.

Oh, man, he had to be so careful not to blow this, not to do anything that would make Sarah Ann realize that, for reasons she could never understand, he didn't remember her. If he hurt her, he'd—

"Don't leave that bed," Patty said, marching into the room carrying a tray. Tucker and Sarah Ann were right behind her. "Dr. Hill said you were to get up only when necessary and since we have meal delivery here, you can prop up against the pillows and eat right there."

"I want to eat with my daddy," Sarah Ann said.

"No, sweetie," Patty said. "You and Tucker are better off up at the table. You can visit your daddy after you finish your sandwich."

David managed to shove the pillows behind him, then leaned against them. Patty put a tray on his lap that held a plate with a sandwich, potato chips, carrot sticks, plus a bowl of rice pudding, and a glass of ice tea.

"Thank you," he said. "This looks great."

"I telled Patty you liked lots of sugar in your ice tea," Sarah Ann said, obviously pleased with herself.

David took a sip of the tea and smiled at his daughter.

"Perfect," he said. This three-year-old little girl knew more about him than he did, which he'd better not dwell on or he'd thoroughly depress himself. "Just right."

"You two go wash your hands and start on your lunches," Patty said. "I'll be right there."

"'Kay," they said, running off.

"Do they ever walk?" David said.

"Not often," Patty said, smiling. "How are you feeling, David? I hated to wake you because you were so sound asleep, but I decided food was important, too."

"The nap did wonders," he said, "and I'm hungry as a bear. I appreciate the lunch and the delivery service."

"Well, holler if you need anything."

"Couldn't you join me in here with your lunch? No, I guess not. You have to supervise the troops." David poked a potato chip that split in two. "I didn't recognize Sarah Ann, Patty. The only reason I knew who she was was due to the picture you brought me. I lied through my teeth and told her that I'd missed her." He looked up at Patty again. "I had to lie to my own daughter."

"That's necessary right now," Patty said gently.

"Yeah, I know but... Well, you'd best go ride herd on those two. Where's Sophia?"

"Snoozing away in her bed." Patty laughed. "If she stays true to form she'll wake up after I've had three bites—maximum—of my sandwich and think she's starving to death.''

"When you laugh or smile," David said, looking at her intently, ''your whole face lights up and your eyes sort of dance, or something. I like the sound of your laughter, too. It reminds me of wind chimes. Well, there's a memory flash for you. I know what wind chimes sound like—your laughter.''

"That's a lovely thing to say," Patty said, feeling a warm flush stain her cheeks. "Wind chimes. Thank you.''

"If I thanked you for everything I'm grateful to you for, I'd run out of oxygen. So, I'll say it once more and hope you know how sincerely I mean it. Thank you, Patty Clark.''

"You're welcome, David Montgomery," she said, hardly above a whisper.

Their gazes met. Blue eyes and dark, dark eyes. Neither of them moved or hardly breathed. Time stopped, the room faded into a hazy mist, then David's hand floated from the bed, palm up, moving toward Patty.

"Mommy," Tucker yelled, racing back into the room. "I spilled my milk.''

Patty jerked and splayed one hand on her racing heart.

"Oh, you startled me, Tucker," she said, dragging her gaze from David's. "I'm coming. Go, go, go.'' She hurried after him as he left the room.

David took a deep breath, then let it out slowly, puffing his cheeks.

Damn it, he thought. Patty was turning him inside out. She wasn't doing it on purpose, he knew that.

She was just being Patty and, heaven help him, he wanted her. The mere image in his mind of kissing her, holding her, then...

He had to gain control of this raging desire that was consuming him. Patty had brought him into her home, trusted him, was helping him do what was best for his daughter.

So what does he do? He fantasizes about making love to Patty for hours and hours, then falling asleep with her nestled in his arms. What a sleazeball he was. His wife had died, for God's sake, and for all he knew he was frozen with grief.

Well, his body sure didn't know it if he was *frozen*. The heat that had consumed him, hot and coiled, when Patty had pinned him in place with those incredible eyes of hers would melt ten tons of icebergs.

Oh, yeah, he had to get control of this before he did something stupid that diminished him in Patty's eyes. He couldn't bear the thought of that. She'd admitted that she didn't really know him as a man, only as a father. Hell, *he* didn't know himself as a man, either. What if he was a scum? A guy who lusted after every lovely woman who crossed his path even though he was supposedly mourning his dead wife? Could he really be that much of a lowlife?

No. Damn it, no. He wasn't like that, was he? Patty was adamant about the fact that he was a devoted and loving father. A decent human being. Did he have a split personality? Was he a great daddy and a hustler of women, too? No, that didn't feel right, didn't...fit, feel comfortable.

His desire for Patty was real, belonged to him. It wasn't tacky, it was honest. But what about his emotions for Sarah Ann's mother? Where were they? What were they?

David sighed, ordered himself to blank his mind for now, somehow, and picked up a carrot stick.

Patty managed to choke down her lunch and comment in all the right places on what Tucker and Sarah Ann were chattering about. Another part of her was listening for Sophia who was due to eat. The majority of her, however, was reliving that unsettling scene in the bedroom when the only two people in the entire universe had been her and David.

Dear heaven, she thought, pushing her plate to one side. The heat. She couldn't remember when she'd been consumed with such heat, such want of a man, of David. The very clothes on her body had felt heavy and hot, urging her to tear them from her burning skin, fling them away so there would be no barriers between her and David when they—

Sophia wailed in the distance.

"Thank goodness," Patty said, jumping to her feet. "Two cookies each from that plate, Tucker, Sarah Ann. You both ate very well."

"I want to go see my daddy," Sarah Ann said.

So do I, Patty thought, then shook her head in self-disgust.

"Finish your cookies and milk, then you can go visit him," she said. "I'll be back. I have to feed the baby."

Patty fed Sophia while sitting in the rocking chair in the nursery. She could hear the deep rumble of David's voice and the giggles of Tucker and Sarah Ann, but couldn't make out what they were talking about. She lifted Sophia to her shoulder and rubbed the baby's back until a tiny burp was heard, then put the infant in her crib. Patty traced the perfect shell-like shape of one of Sophia's ears with her fingertip.

Okay, she thought. She was doing fine now. Calm, cool and collected. She'd simply overreacted when she'd seen David in her bed, that's all. She was a normal, healthy woman and it had been many months since… Well, forget it.

She had no intention of ever becoming involved with a man again, not emotionally, not physically. She was on guard now against David's masculine magnetism. Immune. There. That was a great word. She was back to viewing David as Sarah Ann's father. Not a man, a daddy. The end.

With a decisive nod, Patty left the nursery and went to the master bedroom.

"Okay, short people, it's nap time," she said cheerfully. "Let's go."

"No," Sarah Ann said. "I want to stay with my daddy."

"Sarah Ann," David said, "you must do what Patty tells you. We're all going to take naps now, because, well, because it's nap time."

"Are you going to nap on this bed with my daddy?" Sarah Ann said to Patty.

"Yeah, she is," Tucker said. "This is my mommy's bed. There's lots of room on it so she won't bump your daddy's boo-boo. Right, Mommy?"

"Well, no," Patty said, staring at a space just above Tucker's head. "I'll be sleeping on that bed in Sophia's room while David and Sarah Ann are here with us."

Tucker frowned. "Why?"

"'Cause only a mommy and a daddy sleep in the same bed, Tucker," Sarah Ann said. "That's what my daddy told me when I wanted to sleep with him after I had a bad dream."

"They *are* a mommy and daddy, dumbhead," Tucker said. "So they can sleep together in this bed."

"I am not a dumbhead," Sarah Ann yelled. "You're a dumbhead, Tucker, you are."

"Nap time," Patty said. "Definitely overdue."

"It was an interesting discussion while it lasted," David said, chuckling. He sobered in the next instant when Patty glared at him. "Sorry."

"I'll tuck these charming children in, then get that tray out of your way, David," Patty said.

Patty ended up reading Tucker and Sarah Ann a story to calm them down enough to fall asleep after the excitement of David's arrival on the scene.

When she returned to the master bedroom, the bathroom door was closed and she could hear water running in the sink.

David must be washing up, she thought, retrieving the tray from the bed. Dr. Hill had said that the next lighter-weight cast David would graduate to was a nifty new kind that allowed the injured party to shower, but for now David was limited to sponging off in the sink.

Mmm, she thought. David wasn't all that steady on the crutches yet. Maybe she should wait right here in case he needed help weaving his way back to the bed. Yes, that was a good idea.

She put the tray on top of the dresser, then sat down on the edge of the bed opposite from the side David was using. The water in the bathroom continued to run.

Patty glanced at the beckoning pillow covered by the spread, hesitated, then slipped off her shoes and stretched out with a sigh.

The very second she heard that water stop, she mused, she'd pop right up again and be ready to assist the patient if needed. She'd just relax here for now, just for a few minutes. That water sounded like rain. Soothing. She'd always liked falling asleep to the music of falling rain....

David opened the bathroom door and shuffled his way forward on the crutches, an earthy expletive accompanying his staggering trek. At the edge of the bed he stopped so suddenly he nearly toppled over backward. He steadied, then stared at a sleeping Patty.

Look who's sleeping in my bed, he thought. Forget Goldilocks, that was pretty Patty. Oh, man, what a lovely picture she made. She was on her side, turned toward him, her jean-clad legs bent a bit and her hands tucked beneath her cheek. Her lips...yes, they *were* parted slightly, just as he'd imagined they'd be. She was beautiful.

David's leg began to ache, and as carefully as he possibly could, he placed the crutches on the floor and eased back onto the bed. Patty didn't move. He shifted slightly so he could see her clearly, then watched her, simply watched her sleep.

So peaceful, he thought. The whole house, in fact, had a stillness, an aura of contentment, of all being as it should be as its occupants slept, rejuvenating themselves for the remaining hours of the day. This was a home, not just a house. A real home filled with love and laughter.

Had he created this kind of atmosphere for Sarah Ann in what Patty said was a very large house that he'd purchased? He didn't know.

All he really knew at the moment was that he was inches away from a woman he desired beyond measure. Patty, Patty, Patty. There were so many facets to her, like an exquisite flower with many different petals that fit together to make up the whole.

Patty Clark was a fantastic mother with that magical sixth sense that natural-born mothers had. She was also a caring, thoughtful and very giving woman, as evidenced by the fact that he and Sarah Ann were presently living under her roof.

She was independent and had a feisty temper at times, which he'd provoked at the hospital when he'd been acting like a jerk. And yet there was a vulnerability about her, an aura of innocence that made a man want to stand between her and harm's way, protect her from the harsh realities of the world.

Oh, yes, a complex and enchanting woman was Ms. Patty Clark, David thought. She'd been deeply hurt by her ex-husband, the dud, but she was moving forward with her life, focusing on her children, wrapping her role of mother around herself like a safe and comforting blanket.

David frowned as he continued to gaze at Patty.

She had said, he recalled, that she didn't separate the woman within from the mother, or something like that. Whatever needs, wants, hopes and dreams that Patty the woman might have, she was overshadowing and ignoring them as she performed her duties as a mother.

That was wrong.

He was no expert on the subject but he just knew that was very, very wrong. Who would Patty the woman be when Tucker and Sophia were up and grown and left home? An empty shell who lived for visits and calls from her children? Oh, Patty deserved better than that, needed to embrace the woman within her, allow her to…roar.

David frowned in self-disgust.

Wasn't he just full of himself? There he was deciding how Patty should conduct her life when he didn't have a clue as to how he conducted his own. Yeah, okay, he was a good father. He'd give himself that.

But what kind of a man was he? Did he have a reasonable balance in his life between work and his responsibilities at home? Was he an attorney with a reputation of excellence, or was he just mediocre, one more lawyer in the masses that evoked less-than-flattering jokes?

Had he been a devoted and loving husband to his deceased wife? Was his desire for Patty going to be snuffed out like the flame on a candle when he regained his memory and discovered he was shattered by the loss of his soul mate?

Oh, that didn't seem possible. What he was feeling for Patty was so real, so honest somehow. Each petal of that flower that was her was to be cherished, not shoved roughly aside when his memory returned. He wouldn't do that. Would he? But he really didn't know for certain because the tormenting mystery continued to plague him.

Who was David Montgomery?

Patty stirred and opened her eyes. She smiled at David, a warm, womanly, sleepy smile. Her lashes began to drift down again, but in the next instant, her eyes flew wide open and she sat bolt upward on the bed, staring at David.

"Why are you in my bed?" she said, then shook her head sharply. "No, correct that. Why am I in *your* bed, which is actually my bed, but at the moment it's your bed, and I have no business being here because... How did this happen? Oh, I am mortified, just so-o-o embarrassed."

"Why?" David propped his elbow on the bed and rested his head on the palm of his hand. "You took a little snooze. I don't remember any fine points of the law at the moment, but I find it hard to believe that it's a felony. No harm was done."

"Would you stop and think a minute?" Patty said, scrambling off the bed. "What if the kids had walked in here while I was doing my little snooze number? Huh? What about that, mister?"

"No biggy." David shrugged. "They've already decided that we're eligible to sleep together here because we're a mommy and a daddy...dumbhead."

"Dumbhead," Patty said with a burst of laughter. "Well, I'll count my blessings. It could have been worse. Some of the kids at the Fuzzy Bunny know language you wouldn't believe, let me tell you." She paused and frowned. "I'm getting off the subject. I apologize for falling asleep in...on...your bed."

"It's *your* bed."

"Don't start that again," she said, pointing a finger at him. "This could have been a terrible disaster. If Tucker had seen...and then told my father and Uncle Ryan tonight that you and I... Oh, good grief."

"You've lost me here."

"Oh, that's right," Patty said, "I haven't informed you of that fun newsflash. My father, retired cop that he is, is having a royal fit because you're staying here. He and my uncle Ryan, who also happens to be a retired police officer, are coming over tonight to put you through the third degree, buster."

"That ought to take about three seconds," David said, "seeing how I don't know much more than I like chocolate sauce on my chocolate ice cream and Sarah Ann's favorite television show is *Blue's Clues*. But I take it that your father is a tad upset with this arrangement?"

"That's putting it mildly." Patty sighed. "I love my dad to pieces, but he does have a tendency to forget that I'm a grown woman capable of making my own decisions and dealing with life as it comes. You should have heard him when he found out what Peter... No, that is not a scene I care to recall."

"From what I understand about Peter Clark he justly deserves whatever your father might have dished out."

"Which would have changed nothing, David."

David smiled. "No, but your dad would have felt great during that discussion with Mr. Clark."

"Big macho deal," Patty said, shaking her head. "Listen, maybe my mother will be able to talk my father out of coming over here with Uncle Ryan in tow. But if not, I apologize in advance for what those two might put you through. It's just that…''

''They love you,'' David said quietly.

''Yes. Yes, they do.''

''And that, Patty Clark, is very, very easy to understand.''

Chapter Six

David sat on the sofa in Patty's living room, his injured leg propped on a pillow on the coffee table as he read an article in a newsmagazine. Earlier he had read Sarah Ann and Tucker a story as they snuggled close to him, one on each side, smelling like fresh air and soap from their baths.

Patty had sat in a comfortable chair opposite the sofa while the story was being read, thoroughly enjoying the luxury of having extra time to hold Sophia after feeding her. Prayers were said in the living room so David could hear them, then Patty tucked all three children into bed.

Now at eight-thirty she paced restlessly around the room, while David appeared completely relaxed as he concentrated on the magazine.

"Aren't you nervous?" Patty said finally, stopping in front of him.

"About what?" David said, looking up at her.

"My father and Uncle Ryan coming over here." Patty glanced at her watch for the umpteenth time. "Any second now."

David laughed. "You act like they're going to come in with guns drawn and tell me to get up against the wall and spread 'em."

"One never knows," Patty said, frowning.

"Patty, look," David said, setting the magazine next to him on the cushion. "I..."

The doorbell rang.

"Oh, good grief," Patty said, her hands flying to her cheeks. "There they are."

"Are you going to let them in?"

"Oh." Patty hurried to the door.

Moments later she was introducing her father and uncle to David, who apologized for not rising to shake hands.

Retired or not, David thought, scrutinizing the men, they looked like cops. They were tall, trim, nicely muscled and had that elusive aura of authority about them that would announce their occupations when they walked into a room. And neither one of them was smiling.

Patty fluttered around, telling the guests to sit down, asking if they wanted refreshments which they refused, then giving up and sinking onto a chair, her hands clutched in her lap.

"It's really a pleasure to meet you," David said, smiling.

"Mmm," Ted Sharpe said, frowning.

"I understand you have amnesia from the blow on

the head you suffered in the accident,'' Ryan MacAllister said.

"Correct,'' David said, nodding. "I'm slowly remembering things, but they're trivial, not of any great importance. I have major gaps in my memory that are difficult to deal with. It's pretty depressing to look at a beautiful child like Sarah Ann and have to accept the word of others that she's my daughter.''

"Mmm,'' Ted Sharpe said.

"I'm hoping that you might be able to help me,'' David went on.

"What?'' Ted said, narrowing his eyes.

"I realize that you're both retired police officers,'' David said, "but perhaps you still have contacts on the force. Couldn't you run some sort of background check on me? Find out more facts about who I am?''

Ted leaned forward in his chair. "You *want* us to check you out?''

"I'd sure appreciate it. I know my wife is deceased and has been for quite a while. I'm an attorney and moved to Ventura recently with Sarah Ann from San Francisco. Patty said I have a nice house. Am I renting it? Did I buy it? Is there a firm waiting for me to report to work? Who is David Montgomery? What kind of man am I?''

Ted opened his mouth, then snapped it closed and looked at Ryan, who shrugged.

"What's wrong, Dad?'' Patty said, raising her eyebrows. "Are you surprised by David's request?''

"Well, I... Well...'' Ted cleared his throat. "Okay. Yes, I am. I've already done a background check on you, David, due to the fact that I was very concerned about you being here in Patty's house.''

"That's fair," David said. "I could be a con man, for all you know." He paused. "I'm not, am I?"

Ted pulled a folded piece of paper from the back pocket of his jeans.

"No, you have no criminal record," he said. "Not even a traffic ticket. You were a partner in a law firm in San Francisco called Fisher, Fisher and Montgomery, and sold your partnership to Fisher and Fisher several months ago after being with them for many years. You purchased the house you spoke of. You have excellent credit and are financially sound."

"Dull as dishwater," Ryan said, chuckling.

"What about my wife's death?" David said.

"Hannah told me about that, but we couldn't find anything about a death of a woman with the last name of Montgomery in the San Francisco area in the past several years." Ted shook his head. "Not a thing."

"Can you look further? In other states, or something?" David said.

"Not unless you remember her first name or the date of her death, or something more than we have," Ryan said.

"I don't," David said. "I asked Sarah Ann what her mommy's name was and she just frowned at me and said her name was Mommy. Well, listen, I appreciate your sharing what you found out, although it didn't help much. I can't begin to tell you how upsetting and frustrating this is."

"I'm sorry we couldn't get more information for you," Ted said.

"Dad, you sure are singing a different tune than earlier," Patty said.

"Well, okay, so I made a mistake, sweetheart,"

Ted said. "The story you told us about how David came to be here at your house sounded pretty thin, you know. But now I realize he's on the up-and-up." He paused. "I think I'll have a slice of that cake you offered earlier."

"Make that two, please," Ryan said. "And thank you."

Patty went into the kitchen to prepare the snack, and shook her head as she heard masculine laughter in the distance.

Men, she thought. Now those three were all buddy-buddy. David had handled things perfectly. He had been proactive in regard to a background check, rather than waiting and being put in the less desirable position of having to react to the announcement that his personal history had been examined. Well done, Mr. Montgomery.

But despite the fact that she was glad war hadn't broken out in her living room, it was rather discouraging that no useful information had been discovered about David. And why wasn't there any record of the death of his wife? That was so strange.

Patty carried a tray into the living room and her father jumped to his feet to take it from her. They were all soon enjoying chocolate cake and ice tea.

"What if," Patty said, staring into space, "David contacted this Fisher and Fisher firm and asked them why he sold his partnership and left San Francisco?"

"No," Ted said. "Think about it, Patty. Say a cop moves to a new city, then suddenly calls the station where he had worked before and asks them why he left. He's going to come across as a nutcase and his reputation could be blown. David talking to the Fisher duo is a very, very last resort.''

''Yep,'' Ryan said.

''I understand,'' Patty said. ''I didn't think it through.''

''There were three Fishers at one time,'' David said suddenly. ''Grandfather, father, son. Grandfather retired and I was made a full partner after years of being an associate attorney with them.''

''Go on,'' Patty urged, sitting up straighter in her chair.

''That's it,'' David said. ''I don't know what any of those men look like, or why I left, or...'' He shook his head. ''I never know when I'm going to get a memory flash. It's a bit disconcerting.''

''I guess all you can do is wait it out,'' Ryan said.

''And hope I don't do or say anything that makes it clear to my daughter that I don't really remember her, or the things we've shared.''

''If you blow it,'' Ted said, ''tell her you're having a senior moment.'' He frowned. ''Forget that. You're only thirty-six. At sixty-two, Ryan and I have those moments all the time.''

''Speak for yourself,'' Ryan said. ''My mind is sharp as a tack.''

''Oh, yeah?'' Ted said, laughing. ''And who was that safety-first ex-cop who left the keys in the car when we went golfing last time?''

''That doesn't count,'' Ryan said. ''I was getting into my golf zone, mentally preparing for the game ahead. There wasn't room for things like car keys in my mighty mind.''

The three men laughed and Patty smiled as she swept her gaze from one to the next.

Oh, this was so nice, she thought. She couldn't remember when, if ever, she'd heard so much genuine masculine laughter in this home. Peter had never seemed to really *click* with her family. He'd been a bit overwhelmed by the huge MacAllister clan and had seemed to come across as stiff and aloof at family gatherings.

But David? Now that her father and Uncle Ryan had determined that David wasn't on the ten-most-wanted list, they were all getting along famously, as though they'd known each other for ages.

Which, actually, now that she thought about it, was how she felt about David herself. She liked having him here. Earlier that evening, when he'd been reading to Tucker and Sarah Ann while she had held Sophia, there had been a sense of rightness, warmth, caring in the room.

Peter hadn't enjoyed reading bedtime stories to his son, saying he spent his workday buried in reports and endless stacks of papers, and reading a book was more of the same.

She had such fond memories of being read to by her father and now Tucker was hearing a male voice recite his favorite tales, too. Tucker was definitely going to miss David and Sarah Ann when they returned to their own home, just as she would.

Patty frowned.

Just as she would? she mentally repeated. Maybe it would be best not to examine that statement too closely. Having David and Sarah Ann here was temporary. How she might feel when they left was of little importance, therefore she wouldn't dwell on it. Fine.

Ted picked up the tray containing the empty plates and glasses, bringing Patty from her wandering thoughts.

"I'll put this in the kitchen for you, sweetheart," he said to her. "Then we're out of here."

When Ted returned from the kitchen Ryan and Patty got to their feet.

"I'm glad we came over this evening," Ted said. "My mind is at ease now, David, about your being here. I can understand how difficult it would be to care for your daughter with a broken leg and no memory. Let me know if I can do anything to help out, like take you to the doctor or whatever."

"Thank you," David said. "That would be great because I feel like I'm creating a lot of extra work for Patty and I feel badly about that. I do not, however, have a magical solution to my frustrating problem at the moment."

"Your memory is coming back," Ryan said. "I don't think it's going to take very long to return completely."

"I hope you're right," David said. "I'll be getting a lighter-weight cast soon, too, and that combined with finally remembering who I am and all that goes with it will mean I can take Sarah Ann home where we belong."

"There's no rush, David," Patty said. "We're all doing just fine here." She looked up to see that her father, uncle and David were all staring at her. "What?"

"You sound like you don't want David and his daughter to leave," Ted said.

"Oh, well, I..." Patty said, feeling a warm flush stain her cheeks. "Tucker is certainly enjoying having Sarah Ann here as a playmate, and I have more time for Sophia when David keeps Tucker occupied and...stuff."

"Mmm," Ted said, looking at her for another long moment.

"Let's hit the road," Ryan said.

Patty walked her father and uncle to the door, hugged both, then closed the door behind them with the promise to see them soon. As she turned to walk back to her chair she was acutely aware of the heavy silence in the room.

"That went very well," she said, a little too loudly when she sat back down. "Don't you think so, David?"

"Will you really be sorry when Sarah Ann and I leave?"

"Sure," she said, picking an invisible thread off her jeans. "As I said, Tucker and Sarah Ann are having such fun together and..."

"And you personally?" David interrupted. "Patty the woman, not Patty the mother? How do you feel about us packing up and going to our own home?"

"I've told you, David," she said, frowning. "I don't separate being a mother from being a woman. There's no point in it and I don't intend to do it. Not again. Being a mother is the role, the only role, I center my energies on."

"Why? Why, Patty? Because one man hurt you

very badly so you're labeling all men as scum? Do you think that's fair?''

"I never said that," Patty said, matching his frown. "Peter had his reasons for leaving me and making a life with a woman who meets his needs, and—"

"Wait a minute, wait a minute," David said, raising one hand. "Are you saying that it's *your* fault that Peter deserted his family? *You're* taking responsibility for the breakup of your marriage?"

"I'd rather not discuss this, David," Patty said, getting to her feet. "There's no point in rehashing everything. I know what I know, that's all."

"But—"

"No. Please. Just drop it." Patty crossed the room and turned on the television. "I want to watch the ten-o'clock news."

Was Patty blaming herself for Peter Clark running off with another woman? David thought. Why in the hell would she do that? Peter was the one who had broken their marriage vows, not her. The man was an idiot to have left such a warm, loving and beautiful woman.

So, okay, they'd hit a bump in the wedded-bliss road, but they could have gone for counseling, or something. From where he was sitting there was no excuse for what Peter had done. But for some ridiculous reason, did Patty actually believe it was all her fault? No, that didn't make sense, not one little bit.

"Oh, dear," Patty said, her gaze riveted on the television. "Another bad accident on the freeway. The traffic is a menace on those roads and people drive like maniacs."

"Yeah," David said. "This cast on my leg is proof of that."

"Exactly. This station is doing a special report over the next few weeks about the number of accidents in California and where the worst conditions exist. That's very informative, don't you think?"

"A thrill a minute," David said, rolling his eyes heavenward.

"You're grumpy all of a sudden," Patty said, looking over at him. "You've probably been up too long and you've worn yourself out. Perhaps you should go on to bed and—"

"Damn it, Patty, I am not one of the children you're caring for under this roof. I'm a grown man who is perfectly capable of knowing when he's tired. Do you realize that at dinner you said, 'Tucker, Sarah Ann, David, finish your trees so you can have dessert'? Maybe the kids had trees on their plates, but I was eating broccoli, thank you very much, and I don't need to be bribed with dessert to eat it.

"I don't want to sound ungrateful for what you're doing for me and my daughter, but this being treated like a child could start getting old. I'm a man, Patty. This bit of yours about not separating the woman from the mother is a crock. There's a man living under your roof at the moment and I'd really appreciate carrying on a conversation with a woman, not someone who tells me to eat my trees."

David lifted his injured leg off the pillow and eased it onto the floor. He picked up the crutches from the carpet and leveled himself to his feet.

"Good night," he said. "I apologize if I hurt your

feelings but I had to get that off my chest. I'll see you in the morning."

After David had clomped out of the room, Patty shook her head.

David had definitely gotten overtired, she thought. His leg was probably aching, too, but he refused to take the pain medication the doctor gave him because he said it made him fuzzy. Well, once he tucked himself into bed and slept the night away he'd be his usual chipper self, just like a cranky Tucker was after a much-needed nap. Sure. David...

David was not three years old. David was a man. But she didn't want to view him as a man. No. He was an injured...person whom she was capable of helping by, well, hey, by mothering him a bit. Despite his tantrum on the subject, he was wrong. He didn't need her to perform in the role of a woman, thank goodness, because she didn't have a terrific track record in that arena.

No, David needed mothering, needed to be cared for, have his meals prepared, his clothes washed, a quiet house while he was resting, and on the list went.

Well, she wouldn't get in a snit about what he had said. It had to be difficult for a great big, strong guy like David Montgomery to have to rely on someone the way he was now. She'd humor him a bit, too, and not refer to the broccoli on his plate as trees.

"Ah, the weather report," Patty said, looking at the television again. "A good mother is always aware of what to expect from the weather so she doesn't make plans for her children that can't be carried out because the weather does a switcheroo. Watch that cute little man tell you all about the weather, Patty."

She narrowed her eyes, leaned slightly forward and gave her full attention to the cute little man.

Hours later David lay in bed wide awake, staring up at a ceiling he couldn't see in the darkness. All attempts to fall asleep had failed as his mind replayed over and over the cutting words he'd hurled at Patty.

Where had all that anger come from? he asked himself yet again. He'd felt rotten after he'd hollered his head off, very uncomfortable, which led him to the conclusion that yelling like a lunatic was not something he did on a regular basis.

"Ah, hell," he said, dragging his hands down his face. "I'm losing it."

It had been a nice evening, he mused, once he'd convinced Patty's father and uncle that he was not running some kind of scam on Patty. Ted and Ryan were great guys, fun and funny, intelligent, and he'd thoroughly enjoyed talking with them. They were part of Patty's family and he'd connected, bonded with them, man to man, and could tell that they accepted his staying there with Patty. That had felt good—very, very good.

And that's why he'd gotten so angry.

There it was, finally, clear as a bell. He had no past, was existing the only way he could—in the moment at hand. Once the doubts that Ted and Ryan had about him had been taken care of, they'd all relaxed and enjoyed a pleasant evening. Ted and Ryan had come to visit Patty and David, then eventually said good-night and left, like any normal family.

But once the door had closed behind the two men, he'd been hit with the reality of his situation and he hadn't dealt with the truth of it well at all. He wasn't part of the extended MacAllister clan. He and Patty hadn't welcomed guests into *their* home.

No. He really didn't belong here. He was a temporary addition to the household because Patty felt it was the best thing to do for Sarah Ann. And added to that cold fact was the realization that she was treating him like one more child under her care. The whole scenario had caused him to feel so damn empty, so alone, and he'd lashed out at Patty because she'd told him to eat his trees at dinner.

Well, David thought, at least now he knew why he had been such a jerk. He liked, needed, wanted to be part of a family like the MacAllisters, but he wasn't. Maybe he had relatives somewhere, but he had the feeling he didn't. Somehow he knew that he and Sarah Ann were it, just the two of them.

David yawned and told himself firmly to shut off his mind and go to sleep.

But...

Why was Patty so adamant about not separating the woman from the mother? Surely she was intelligent enough to know that not all men were like Peter Clark. She seemed determined to spend the coming years focused on her children. And when Tucker and Sophia were up and grown? Patty apparently knew that her attitude meant she would spend the remainder of her days alone. Why would she do that to herself? Peter was the villain in this scenario, not Patty. Why couldn't she see that, realize she deserved to be loved, cherished, treated as the wonderful woman that she was?

Questions, questions, questions, David thought. He

had a million of them regarding himself and what he didn't know about David Montgomery. Now he was adding questions about Patty to the teetering tower of unknowns. Damn.

David drifted off to sleep, but was plagued by disturbing and confusing dreams that made no more sense than his own existence.

David came to the table the next morning at breakfast and attempted to apologize to Patty again for his outburst of the previous night.

"Don't give it another thought," Patty said breezily. "This is a new day, you're well rested now, so onward and upward. Are you sure you want to eat out here? I'd be happy to bring you a tray in bed."

"This is fine," David said. He was well rested now, so his naughty behavior of last night was forgiven and forgotten? She was *still* treating him like a child, damn it. "Eating in bed gets lonely very quickly. I prefer to come to the table…like the man of the house."

Patty placed a glass of orange juice in front of David, then stared at him, her head cocked slightly to one side.

"The man of the… Oh," she said. "Well, I…"

Tucker and Sarah Ann came running into the kitchen and climbed onto their chairs.

"Good morning," David said, smiling at the pair. "You must be the baby bears. Patty is the mama bear, and I'm the daddy bear."

"Is Sophia Goldilocks?" Tucker said.

"Works for me," David said.

"Okay," Tucker said. "Daddy bear. This is cool."

"Cool," Sarah Ann said.

"Remember that it's just a game," Patty said quickly. "David is not your daddy, Tucker."

"Sure he is," Tucker said, "'cause I'm a baby bear. Can I have juice like my daddy bear?"

"Me, too," Sarah Ann said.

"Yes, I'll get you both some juice," Patty said, then glared at David, who smiled at her pleasantly.

Much to Patty's steadily growing annoyance, David continued to remind Sarah Ann and Tucker of their baby bear status and his own daddy bear title through the morning and during lunch. When the little ones went down for a nap in the early afternoon, David sat with his leg propped up on the coffee table reading a mystery he'd found on the bookshelf in the living room.

"David," Patty said, sitting down in the easy chair across from him.

"Hmm?" he said, turning the page in the book.

"Would you put that book aside for now? I need to speak to you."

David did as instructed, then looked at Patty questioningly.

"I'd prefer that you dropped this bear game you're playing with the kids," she said, folding her hands in her lap.

"Why?"

"Because you are *not* Tucker's daddy bear. I mean, his daddy, his father. He's already had his heart broken by Peter leaving and rarely visiting him. I don't want that to happen again when you and Sarah Ann go home. Your insisting on the title of daddy bear is very risky emotionally for my son. Do you understand?''

''Are you saying that you don't want Sarah Ann and Tucker to be friends, see each other, have play dates after I get my memory back?''

''Of course they'll be friends, but until I go back to teaching I can't afford to take Tucker to the Fuzzy Bunny where Sarah Ann will be. It won't be that easy for them to be together.''

''In other words, once I remember who I am, you're dusting me off,'' David said, frowning. ''So in the meantime, I shouldn't be Tucker's daddy bear.''

''I'm sure you'll be busy once you remember where you work. Besides, you won't need me for anything at that point, and I can't allow Tucker to get too attached to you so the daddy bear thing isn't a good idea.''

''Mmm. Are you uncomfortable with your title of mama bear? If I'm the daddy bear and you're the mama bear, then you're my wife. You're a *woman* bear as well as a mother to the baby bears.''

''I am *not* a woman bear,'' Patty said. ''Oh, this is a ridiculous conversation. Just knock off the bear thing.''

''No, I like it. It's fun. Ah, come on, Patty, lighten up. It's just a game, a let's-pretend number. No harm will come from it. When the kids get tired of it, we'll move on to something else.''

''I don't want to be a woman bear,'' Patty said, jumping to her feet.

''Fine,'' David said, frowning. ''You can be Goldilocks if that is less threatening to you.''

"What do you mean?"

"You're so terrified of the woman within you that you won't even play a game where you have that title," David said, looking directly at her. "That makes absolutely no sense whatsoever, Patty."

"Yes, it does," she said, wrapping her hands around her elbows. "It does."

"Why? Help me out here. Explain it to me."

"No. I'm going to go make a grocery list."

Patty hurried out of the room and David narrowed his eyes as he watched her leave.

Okay, he thought, Patty won that round. He'd got information zip and zero. But he wasn't finished with his quest to find the answer to his question of why Patty refused to embrace her own womanliness, her femininity, not by a long shot.

He should, he supposed, be concentrating on all the unanswered questions about himself, trying to fill the void within him, and he would do that.

But for some reason that he couldn't even begin to understand, it was very, very important to him to know why Patty Clark refused to be anything other than a devoted mother.

What terrified her so much about being a woman?

Chapter Seven

The remainder of the week seemed to fly by.

David was contacted by the insurance company representing the man who had struck the SUV and a packet of paperwork was delivered by messenger for David to tend to.

He also spent a great deal of time poring over the newspaper ads for vehicles, looking for the best buy.

On Wednesday, David remembered that he liked green grapes but not purple ones, his favorite color was blue and he was allergic to goose-feather bed pillows.

On Thursday his memory dished up the information that Sarah Ann had been born with a fuzzy cap of blond hair which fell out later, and the replacement crop had been the silky, black curls she now had. He had a sudden flash of a woman's face, but it was gone so quickly he hadn't been able to discern anything other than the fact that she was very angry.

On Friday he told Patty he enjoyed taking part in a pickup game of basketball or football, but didn't like golf because it was much too slow. He preferred his steaks rare, roast beef medium and bacon that was crisp to the point of being nearly burned.

"I haven't remembered one useful bit of data," David said on Saturday afternoon while the children napped.

"All this is dumb stuff. I mean, isn't it exciting to learn that I like bacon that's cooked to the consistency of shoe leather?" He shook his head. "I'm going crazy here."

Patty sat down on the sofa next to David, who was in his usual pose with his leg propped on a pillow on the coffee table. She placed one hand on his shoulder.

"It *is* important information, David," she said, "for the simple reason that you remembered it. Your memory is returning a little bit at a time, that's all. It's like when Tucker was learning his colors. We started with red and blue, then added more as he—"

"That's it." David shifted so he could grip Patty's shoulders with both hands. "There's another 'let's compare David to a child' number. Do you realize that you actually patted me on the head when I remembered that I liked green grapes? Clapped your hands after my goose-feather announcement?

"Damn it, Patty, I…am…a…man. What is it going to take to get you to… Ah, hell."

And with that, David Montgomery kissed Patty Sharpe Clark.

Patty's first reaction was such complete shock that

she stiffened and her eyes widened, but in the very next instant her lashes drifted down. She realized in some deep inner place that she had been waiting for this kiss, yearning for it, fantasizing about what it might be like to be kissed by David.

And it was ecstasy.

She blanked her mind, refusing to think about the right or wrong of it, and just savored the exquisite sensations swirling throughout her. She could feel the pulse of heat low in her body and welcomed it, recognized it as desire a step beyond anything she had experienced before. A whimper whispered from her throat as she returned David's kiss in total abandon.

Oh, yes, David thought hazily, as he slipped his tongue into the sweet darkness of Patty's mouth. They'd been moving toward this kiss, the tension and awareness growing more acute with every passing day. It had been an eternity but now, oh, now, Patty the woman was receiving his kiss, holding nothing back, kissing him in return.

David broke the kiss only long enough to take a raspy breath, then slanted his mouth in the other direction. He wrapped his arms around Patty to bring her closer, felt her breasts press against his chest as she encircled his neck with her hands.

The kiss went on and on, and the heat within them coiled tighter, lower, as passion consumed them. There was no world, no children, no worries or woes, no unanswered questions, nothing beyond the two of them. And this kiss.

David began to feel his self-control slipping to the edge. Slowly and so reluctantly, he gripped Patty's shoulders again and eased her back from his aroused body, his breathing labored.

Patty sighed softly, then lifted her lashes to gaze into David's eyes, now a smoky hue that radiated the message of his desire.

"I..." she started, then stopped as she realized there were no further words available in the sensuous mist in her mind.

"Patty," David said, his hands still holding her shoulders. "Don't say that shouldn't have happened. Okay? Because it was destined to happen, was due and overdue."

"But—"

"You can talk from here to Sunday about how you don't separate the woman from the mother within you—" he went on, his voice gritty with need "—but you and I both know now that isn't true." He smiled. "That kiss was Patty the woman and David the man, pure and simple."

"There's nothing simple about it, David," Patty said, an echo of sadness in her voice. "It's terribly, terribly complicated. I don't *want* the woman part of me to be a separate entity. I don't.

"And you? Oh, David, don't you see? Your wife is dead and you don't know what emotions you're dealing with about that. We're not free, either one of us, to give way to this desire we feel for each other. Or maybe it's only lust. Heavens, I don't know. I just... Oh, dear."

"You're working up to saying this shouldn't have happened," David said, frowning. "And I'm not going there. I refuse to. I'm living my life a minute at a time, waiting for my memory to return and now, right now, what we just shared was so right and so damn sensational."

"But there's nothing wrong with *my* memory," Patty said, "and I know that—"

"That you were hurt very badly by your ex-husband," David interrupted. "I understand that."

"No, you don't understand."

"Listen to me. This might sound crazy, but hear me out. I don't know what I'll be facing when my memory slams back into place. We do know it's been more than a year or two since my wife died and I can't believe that I might feel guilty about getting on with my life.

"I'm living in…in a bubble of sorts, a limbo state where all I can do is act and react to the moment at hand. Come with me, Patty, into my sphere, take some time off from the pain you suffered, the hurt and betrayal you've had to deal with and just be. With me. Just be."

"Oh, David, that is so dangerous," she said, shaking her head. "You're burying that bubble in the sand where reality can't touch it, but that sand is going to be swept away when you remember what you've temporarily forgotten."

"And we know that, so we can't get hurt," he said. "Why can't I hold you, kiss you, fill the emptiness within me with you? Why can't you hold me, kiss me, push aside your pain and bask in the warmth of sharing and caring for as long as it lasts?

"We're intelligent adults. We know the facts as they stand. Can't we grab hold of what we have together and savor it while we can? Don't we deserve to just *be* for however long we have?"

Oh, dear heaven, Patty thought, why was what David was saying making sense, seeming so reasonable, when it was actually bordering on insane?

But, oh, to have a reprieve from the truth of her failings, to move the woman apart from the mother and allow that woman once again to rejoice in her femininity. Just for a little while. Could she do that? Yes, darn it, she could. And David was right. They deserved, both of them, a respite from the turmoil in their minds. Just for a little while.

"Patty?"

She nodded slowly. "Just for a little while. We can't get hurt because we know the facts, know this is all temporary, a gift we're giving ourselves because we need to replenish our strength to move on. We need to just be. For a little while."

"Are we crazy?" David said, smiling.

"Oh, there's no doubt about that," Patty said, laughing. "But I don't care. I do think we should be very careful around Tucker and Sarah Ann because we don't want them to be disappointed, upset, whatever, when we go our separate ways. They've both been through enough, just as we have."

"Agreed."

"I've never entertained the idea of having an...an affair in my entire life."

"Forget the word *affair* because that's tacky," David said. "I like how you put it before. This is a gift we're giving to ourselves."

"A gift. Yes, that's much nicer, softer." Patty nodded. "All right, David, it *is* crazy, but no one is going to be hurt by this decision. We're just doing an adult time-out from the turmoil of our lives."

"Well put."

"Except I can't make love with you."

"What?" he said. "Why not?"

"David, I have a month-old baby. I haven't been cleared by my doctor to engage in…you know."

"Oh, yeah, I forgot about that. And I have a cumbersome cast on my leg that…" David laughed. "What a pair we are. Well, special things are worth waiting for, or however that saying goes."

"You might regain your memory before we're able to…"

"Shh. We're living in the moment, remember? And in this moment at hand I'm going to kiss you again before Sarah Ann and Tucker wake up from their naps."

"Good idea."

The kiss ignited all the heat and passion of the one before, but now there was more. There was a sense of anticipation of what was yet to come intertwined with the desire.

There was a depth of understanding, of rightness, of knowing they would cherish this gift they had given themselves, and the memories of all they would share would be theirs to do with as they wished. They were in a place where neither had been before but it was theirs. And it was good. Just for a little while.

That night David decided he wanted to eat with the others and managed to prop his leg on a chair beneath the table. The menu was hamburgers, fries and juicy chunks of delicious cantaloupe.

"How come you're smiling so much, Mommy?"

Tucker said, then put three pieces of fruit in his mouth.

"Eat those one at a time, Tucker," Patty said. "I didn't realize I was smiling *so much,* but if I am it means I'm a happy person."

"Oh?" David said, raising his eyebrows. "And just what is causing this sudden euphoria?"

Patty glared at David, who immediately hooted with laughter.

"Happy person?" Tucker said. "Are you done crying and stuff 'bout Daddy?"

"I cried about Daddy?" Patty said.

"Lots and lots," Tucker said, nodding. "I told Grandma and she said that mommies get to cry when they get sad just like kids do."

"That doesn't work so good," Sarah Ann said, frowning. "If mommies and daddies cry, who's going to hug them and make them feel better?"

Tucker shrugged. "Don't know."

"A daddy could hug a mommy," David said, "and a mommy could hug a daddy."

"We don't have a daddy," Tucker said.

"We don't have a mommy," Sarah Ann said. "I told you this doesn't work so good."

"Okay, try this," David said. "While we're living here, Sarah Ann, I'll hug Patty if she gets sad and she'll hug me if I get sad. Does *that* work for you?"

"Guess so," Sarah Ann said.

"'Kay," Tucker said.

"But I don't think you have to worry about Patty or me being sad," David said, then shifted his gaze to Patty.

"That's right, David," Patty said. "No more tears."

"But what about when you don't live here no more?" Tucker said.

"*Any* more," Patty corrected. "Don't worry about that, Tucker. What book shall we read at bedtime tonight?"

"I want my daddy to tell me his own story," Sarah Ann said, "'bout the brown dragon who wants to be red 'cause he likes red bestis. 'Kay, Daddy?"

David stiffened slightly. "I... Um... Wouldn't you rather I read a story you haven't heard before?"

"No," Sarah Ann said. "I want the one you thinked up in your head about the dragon."

"I have a better idea," Patty said, seeing the frantic expression on David's face; he didn't have a clue what the dragon tale was. "Why don't you tell the dragon story to all of us at bedtime, Sarah Ann? That would be fun."

"Fantastic," David said, then let out a pent-up breath.

Sarah Ann nodded slowly. "I could do that. 'Kay."

The meal was finished, then the children were excused with permission to watch one *Blue's Clues* video. Patty began to clear the table.

"Thanks for bailing me out on the dragon story," David said, stacking the dishes within his reach. "I wonder what I named the poor drab brown creature."

"Sarah Ann will tell us," Patty said, smiling.

"We make a good team, Patty," David said, looking directly at her. "I fumbled the ball, you picked it up and slam-dunked it. Yep, a very good team."

"For a little while," Patty said softly, then turned and walked to the counter with more dishes.

"Yeah," David said, then frowned as he fiddled with a spoon, lost in his own thoughts.

At bedtime Sarah Ann told the story of the dragon, whose named turned out to be Max and was able to turn red by finding a magic garden of strawberries and eating every one. Tucker was enchanted by the tale, but David told Patty that he didn't think he should quit his day job to become a writer of children's stories.

On the late news there was another segment of the series dealing with high automobile accident areas in California. The focus that evening was on Orange County.

"I hope this report helps the situation," Patty said, "because it's rather depressing to watch." She paused. "Well, I'm going to get ready for bed."

Per their usual routine, Patty used the bathroom off the master bedroom while David was still in the living room. Once she was finished and in the nursery, David would make his clumsy way down the hall.

Standing before the bathroom mirror above the sink in her full-length cotton nightgown, Patty stared at her reflection.

She didn't look any different, she thought. There was her dark hair and her nice but rather ordinary features. But she *felt* different, more aware of her own body, her breasts, the feminine slope of her hips, the softness of her skin.

Because of David.

People, her family included, would no doubt highly disapprove of her wanton decision to have a short-term affair with David Montgomery. No, no, not an affair. It was a gift they were giving themselves and no one around them would ever know, or be in a position to pass judgment.

She would have no regrets about what she had done when it was over. None. She would savor the memories and once again function only in the role of mother in the years ahead. The lonely years ahead. Without David.

Patty shook her head sharply in self-disgust at where her thoughts had taken her, then left the bathroom to find David already sitting on the edge of the bed.

"Oh, you startled me," she said.

"I wanted to say a proper good night to you." David patted the space next to him. "Would you sit next to me here?"

Patty settled on the bed next to David, shifting slightly so she could look directly at him.

"Ah, Patty," he said, taking her left hand in both of his. "When Sarah Ann was telling the story about Max the dragon it really hit me hard that I'm a lousy father at the moment. I can't even remember a special story I made up for my daughter.

"Is she due for a dental checkup or a yearly physical at the doctor? Are there vitamins somewhere in my house that she should be taking? Do we have something special we do together on the weekends when it's just the two of us living under the same roof? Maybe I make her pancakes for breakfast, or take her to the park, or—"

"David, don't do this to yourself," Patty interrupted. "I know it's frustrating not to be able to remember the kind of things you're talking about, but your memory is coming back. You know it is. You have to be patient.''

''Ignore me.'' David sighed. ''I'm feeling sorry for myself as well as being so terrified that I'm going to let Sarah Ann down somehow. I would have tonight if you hadn't bailed me out about the story. Can you imagine the look on her face if I had said I didn't remember anything about Max the dragon?''

''But that didn't happen.''

''Thanks to you.''

Patty smiled. ''Well, you did say we're a good team. I'm getting very spoiled having such lovely extra time to hold Sophia, and being able to fix dinner without Tucker's help because you're keeping him entertained.''

''You're right,'' he said, releasing her hand and framing her face with his hands. ''We *are* a good team. A very...'' He lowered his head slowly toward Patty's. ''...good...'' He brushed his lips over hers, causing a shiver to course through her. ''...team.''

David's mouth melted over Patty's as she leaned into the kiss, wrapping her arms around his back. The heat of desire suffused them instantly, burning with an intensity that seemed to steal the very breath from their bodies. When they ended the kiss their breathing was labored and their hearts were racing.

''Whew,'' David said. ''You are turning me inside out, lady.''

''You're rather overwhelming yourself, sir.'' Patty drew a much-needed breath. ''Gracious.'' She got to her feet. ''Good night, David.''

''Good night, Chet.''

She laughed in delight at his silliness, then her smile softened.

"Sleep well," she said, then left the room.

"Right," David said dryly, to the empty room. "I need a cold shower, but I have to settle for a cold sponge bath. Hell."

In the middle of the night David woke suddenly and sat bolt upward in bed, his heart pounding, sweat running down his chest.

Whoa, he thought. Calm down, Montgomery. He'd had a nightmare, that's all, but it had been so vivid, so real, so... There had been a woman with blond hair whose face he couldn't discern. Even though he couldn't see her clearly he knew she was angry, raging with fury, and she was walking away, carrying Sarah Ann. But it was a younger Sarah Ann, maybe a year or so old.

He had been frantic, reaching for his daughter, but the woman kept going and he couldn't keep up. It didn't matter if the woman left, but he had to get his precious baby away from her. Then the woman had stopped, put Sarah Ann down, then disappeared. He'd been moving toward Sarah Ann, feeling as though he was losing ground with every step he took. Sarah Ann was crying, holding up her arms to him, as he struggled to get to her and...

"God," David said, dragging shaking hands down his face.

He flopped back onto the pillow, his arms landing with a thud next to him on the bed.

Who was that woman in the dream? he thought frantically. His wife? Sarah Ann's mother? Where had she been going and why didn't he care if she went as long as she didn't take the baby? What had Marsha been so angry about and...

"Marsha?" he said aloud. "Marsha. Marsha Welsh Montgomery. My...my wife."

Chapter Eight

In the middle of the next afternoon, David managed to produce yet another smile, realizing that they were beginning to feel as phony as a three-dollar bill.

"It's a pleasure to meet you, Jessica," he said. "I have, in fact, met quite a few members of the MacAllister family today."

Jessica laughed as she sat down in an easy chair across the room from David.

"What can I say?" she said, still smiling. "Word is out that you're bunked in here with Patty and we could only hold ourselves back for so long."

"I understand," David said. "Let's see. Jessica. You're one of the triplets, right?"

"Right," she said. "I'm married to Daniel who is a police detective and we have Tessa and our newest addition, Danny, who was born in May. The kiddies are home with Daddy at the moment." She paused. "Patty, how's Sophia?"

"Growing like a weed," Patty said from where she sat on the opposite end of the sofa from David. "Time is passing too quickly. I'm hoping to get a teaching job in January, but the thought of leaving Tucker and Sophia all day is so hard to deal with."

"I'm sure it is," Jessica said, nodding. "You've always loved staying home with Tucker and, well, life sometimes brings sad changes that we just have to go with."

"That's true," Patty said quietly.

"Well, I'd better head home," Jessica said, getting to her feet. "I have some groceries in the car. I hope you get your memory back soon, David. It must be awful not remembering the past."

"Mmm," he said. He knew his wife's name now and the fact that she had been very angry about something. He hadn't had an opportunity to tell Patty yet because the visitors had started arriving right after breakfast. "I'm just taking things a day at a time. This is Sunday and I'm meeting a whole bunch of MacAllisters."

Jessica laughed. "Aren't we awful? Who has been here today so far?"

"Well, I met your grandparents, Margaret and Robert," David said. "Then your sister Emily stopped by with a baby girl in tow. She didn't stay long because she and her husband were going to go watch their son in a swimming competition at the high school. Who else? Oh, yes, a pretty pregnant lady named Carolyn. She's married to…wait a minute…oh, yeah, Patty's brother, who is out of town."

"This is getting embarrassing," Jessica said, laughing merrily. "We should have just rented a truck and pounced on you all at once."

"I'm surviving this, I think, although I'm sure my ears should be buzzing from all the talk about me once the guests leave."

"You'd better believe it," Jessica said. "But I'll go home and report to Daniel that you're a very nice man who has a sweetie pie for a daughter. She is so cute. Sarah Ann and Tucker look enough alike to be brother and sister."

"You're not the first to say that," Patty said. "They have the same coloring."

"So do you and David," Jessica said. "No one would guess you're not the parents of this brood because even Sophia has dark hair. Well, I'm off. 'Bye for now."

Patty saw Jessica to the door, then returned to sit on the sofa.

"I'm sorry about this, David," she said, turning her head to look at him. "You must feel like a bug under a microscope." She paused. "I'd better go check on Tucker and Sarah Ann. Putting them down for a nap right after Jessica arrived might mean they're still wired up and getting into mischief in there."

"Okay," David said. "Do you think that's the end of the company for today?"

"Heaven only knows," Patty said, laughing as she left the room.

David watched her go, shifted his leg to a more comfortable position on the pillow, then stared into space.

How should he say this to Patty? he thought. Hey, guess what, my wife's name was Marsha and I don't think she was thrilled to be with me.

David dragged a restless hand through his hair.

He should be pleased, he knew, that he'd remembered something as momentous as his wife's name, but he couldn't shake off the disturbing dream he'd had about how angry she'd been.

Of course, dreams were often images mixed together and making little sense. It wasn't etched in stone as gospel truth that Marsha had been upset just because he'd dreamed that she was.

But he sensed, just somehow knew, that before Marsha had died, things had not been going well in their marriage. What had been wrong, he didn't know at this point.

"Tucker and Sarah Ann are snoozing like little angels," Patty said, coming back into the room carrying Sophia. "I snatched up this miss just as she was beginning to fuss for something to eat so she wouldn't wake the other two."

"Why don't you let me hold her while you warm her bottle?" David said.

"Really?"

"Sure. I know you're a whiz at preparing a bottle while juggling an infant because I've seen you do it, but make it easier on yourself. Hey, Sophia, truck on over here."

Patty laughed. "She comes complete with delivery service." She crossed the room and placed Sophia in David's arms. "Back in a flash."

David stared at the baby tucked in the crook of his arm. Sophia stared right back at him.

"Hi," David said. "You sure are cute. No, you're pretty, just like your mommy. Very, very pretty. So. How's life?"

Sophia puckered up, blew a tiny bubble, then stuck her tongue out at David, who laughed in delight.

"Oh, yeah?" he said, chuckling. "And just what are your complaints, madam? From where I'm sitting you've got it extremely cushy around here. You have your mom trained very well already."

"Here we go," Patty said, returning with a bottle in hand. "I'll take her now, David."

"Could I feed her?" he said.

"Well, I… Yes. Why not?"

Patty handed David the bottle, then turned and went to sit in the easy chair where Jessica had been. She smiled as David poked the bottle in Sophia's mouth.

"You look like a pro at that," she said.

"Maybe I fed Sarah Ann a lot," he said. "I feel very comfortable doing this." He paused and looked over at Patty. "I…I had a dream last night, woke up and couldn't go back to sleep for hours."

"A dream about what?" Patty said, frowning.

"My wife. Her name was Marsha. Marsha Welsh Montgomery."

"Oh. Well. That's great, David, that you remembered something of such importance." Patty attempted to produce a smile that failed to materialize. "Really…terrific."

"You don't sound thrilled, Patty."

"I'm just surprised, that's all," she said. "Your wife has been sort of a cloudy figure but now she has a name. I believe you're very close to remembering everything, David.''

"Maybe. When do I burp this kiddo?"

"Not yet."

"Patty, in the dream Marsha was very angry. She was walking away from me carrying Sarah Ann, a younger Sarah Ann, then suddenly she put the baby down and disappeared. I was trying to get to Sarah Ann but...I've had flashes of a woman before and she was always furious, upset. I think perhaps Marsha and I were having problems in our marriage before she died. I don't know.''

"Or maybe she was angry in the dream," Patty said, "because you were very happy together and she didn't want to leave you but knew she was going to because of an illness or whatever. Dreams can be interpreted many ways.''

"Your theory is interesting, but I don't think it's on the mark," he said. "I get very unsettling vibes, for the lack of a better word, when I center on Marsha. I don't want her here, in this home, where there's sunshine and happiness and... Ah, I'm not making any sense.''

"Yes, you are," Patty said quietly, "because as wrong and selfish as it is, I don't want her here, either. We have this gift we agreed to share together and there's no room for Marsha, for the truth of your reality. Oh, I sound like a terrible person. We should be cheering about the fact that you remembered her.''

"Hooray," David said dryly.

"Shame on you," Patty said, smiling. "That came across like 'Hooray, I'm going to have a root canal.'''

"Because seeing her in the dream, feeling that an-

ger coming from her in waves made me uncomfortable, as if a dark cloud was hanging over my head.
Damn, this is all so confusing.'' David looked at Sophia. "You didn't hear me say damn.''

"Was Marsha...beautiful in your dream?''

"I couldn't see her face clearly enough to know,''
he said, looking at Patty again. "She had blond hair
though.''

"Yet Sarah Ann has dark hair like you.''

"Everyone in this house has dark hair,'' David
said, "and it's been pointed out more than once that
we look like a family with the same coloring. Marsha
doesn't fit in.''

"Don't say that, David. She was your wife. She
was Sarah Ann's mother. The three of you were a
family.''

"A family where the wife and mother was very,
very angry about something.''

"You don't know that for certain,'' Patty said. "It
was a dream, David. I think it would be best not to
dwell on that anger you sensed, saw, and wait until
you remember more.'' She paused. "Sophia needs to
be burped now.''

David set the bottle on the end table, then lifted
the baby to his shoulder and patted her back. Sophia
produced a very unladylike burp.

"Definitely a pro,'' Patty said, smiling at him.
"You're a good daddy.''

"Yeah, but what kind of husband was I?''

Probably far, far better in that role than she had
been in her role as a wife, Patty thought. David didn't
know for certain that Marsha's anger in the dream
was directed at him. But there was no erasing the

stark fact that Peter had left her because she had failed him as a wife.

"Don't torture yourself with guessing games," she said, getting to her feet. "Be patient. Wait for your memory to come back completely. You'll know the truths soon enough."

"Yeah, you're right." David settled Sophia back down, then offered her the bottle again. "Look at her go. You're a little piggy, Sophia. That's good stuff, huh? Your mom is a great cook."

"Who is going to go put a chicken in the oven if you don't mind finishing feeding her."

"Take your time," David said. "I'm enjoying every minute of this."

Patty started toward the kitchen, then stopped and looked back at the pair on the sofa.

What a lovely picture they made, she thought. Father and daughter sharing a special time together. The big strong man holding the fragile baby who was so safe in his arms and… Oh, Patty, shut up.

She spun around and hurried out of the room.

"Tucker, Sarah Ann," Patty said, the next morning at breakfast. "Grandma Hannah is coming over to take care of you and Sophia in a little while. Grandpa Ted is going to take David to the doctor to have a checkup on his leg, and I'm going to my doctor to have a checkup on me."

"Did you break yourself like my daddy broke his leg?" Sarah Ann said.

"No," Patty said, laughing. "I'm sure you've had

check-ups, Sarah Ann, just to be sure everything was all right.''

''Did I, Daddy?'' Sarah Ann said. ''Get checked up?''

''I... Sure, you did,'' David said, not looking directly at her. ''And you're fine, healthy as a horse.''

''I'm not a horse,'' she said, giggling. ''I'm a girl.''

''Really?'' David said, peering at her. ''Well, so you are, and a very pretty one, too. And you're very handsome, Tucker.''

''Kay,'' he said, shrugging.

''When you're a teenager that will matter to you, Tucker,'' David said, laughing. ''Big-time.''

''Trevor's a teenager,'' Tucker said. ''He's the bestis swimmer you ever saw. We went with Aunt Emily and Uncle Mark to watch Trevor swim and he won the race. When I gets to be a teenager and can swim good will you watch me in the water, David?''

''That's a long time from now, Tucker,'' David said quietly.

''Yeah, but will you be there to watch me swim good?'' Tucker said.

''I can't promise that, Tucker,'' David said, ''but if it's humanly possible I'll be there.''

''Kay,'' Tucker said. ''Can I have a banana, Mommy?''

''Magic word,'' Patty said.

''Please,'' Tucker said.

''One banana coming right up,'' Patty said.

Patty peeled the banana and began to cut it into bite-size pieces by rote, her mind centered on the conversation between Tucker and David about an audience when Tucker was swimming way down the road.

Tucker was getting so attached to David, she thought. She'd invited David to stay here until his

memory returned because it was the best thing for
Sarah Ann. But had she made the wrong decision in
regard to her son? Had she made a tremendous mistake in her role of mother?

Tucker had lost one father when Peter left them.
Would her little boy feel deserted and betrayed again
when David and Sarah Ann went to their own home?
Would Tucker cry when David left, miss him so much
it was heartbreaking?

Dear heaven, she couldn't bear the thought of
Tucker weeping in her arms. And she couldn't bear
the thought of it being her fault, a glaring error she
performed as a mother. If she proved inadequate in
that role she would have nothing left, would be an
empty shell.

No. Now stop. David and Sarah Ann weren't going
to disappear off the face of the earth. The kids could
have play dates, and when she went back to teaching
they'd see each other every day at the Fuzzy Bunny.

Sure, Tucker would miss the Montgomerys when
they first left, but he'd soon come to see that they
were still a part of his life. Fine.

A part of *Tucker's* life, she thought, as she placed
the plate of banana bites in front of him. But David
would no longer be a part of *her* life. The gift they
had agreed to share was temporary, would end when
David took his daughter home. She knew that.
Wanted it that way. She had nothing more to offer
than the short-term gift—also known as an affair—
while David was living under her roof. So be it.

She would miss David when he left and Sarah Ann,
too, of course, just as Tucker would, but she certainly
wouldn't cry about their going. She was an adult who

understood the facts of the situation and was prepared to deal with them in a mature manner. Right?

"Right," she said, not realizing she'd spoken aloud.

"Right?" David said with a burst of laughter. "Are you sure, or would you like to reconsider your answer?"

"What?" Patty said. "I'm sorry. I was mentally off somewhere. What did I just agree to?"

"Tucker said," David said, smiling, "that if a family wanted a puppy it would be bestis to get one puppy for each person so they'd didn't have to share it, take turns playing with it."

Patty's eyes widened. "Oh, good grief. Tucker, honey, no. One puppy per family is quite enough."

"'Kay," he said. "Can we get a puppy?"

"No, sweetheart, we can't," she said. "It wouldn't be fair to that little bundle because he'd be alone all day."

Tucker frowned. "We're here all day."

"I know, but after Christmas, Mommy is going to be teaching school while you go to the Fuzzy Bunny and Sophia goes to a place that tends to babies, and we won't be here all day anymore." Patty smiled. "See?"

"You won't be at the Fuzzy Bunny with me?" Tucker said, his voice rising. "You were there before and I could talk to you and get hugs and...I don't want to be there without you, Mommy. I don't. I don't. No, no, no."

"Sarah Ann will be there, Tucker," David said.

"I don't care. I want my mommy with me at the Fuzzy Bunny." Tucker's bottom lip began to tremble.

"This topic should never have gotten this far," Patty said. "Tucker, please don't be upset. All of that is so far away in the future. It's nothing we have to worry about now. Let's just enjoy today, okay? Oh, look at the time. Grandma Hannah will be here very soon and you know how much fun you have with her."

"Grandma Hannah can make hats from paper folded," Tucker said. "Cool."

"Very cool," Patty said. "You can make a hat for you and Sarah Ann and a little bitty one for Sophia."

"We'll put stickers on the hats," Tucker said. "I gotta find my stickers." He slid off his chair. "Come on, Sarah Ann, we gotta look for the stickers."

"'Kay," she said, wiggling off her chair. "I want some stickers on my hat, too."

As the pair ran from the room, Patty sank onto a chair with a sigh.

"Oh, my," she said, shaking her head. "Shades of things to come. Tucker is going to have a difficult adjustment being at the Fuzzy Bunny without me. I hate this."

"You'd do well to take your own advice," David said. "Enjoy today."

"I know, but I'm starting to get the applications for teaching positions in the mail that I requested over the phone. I'll have no choice but to face the stark facts every time I fill one out and mail it back. I can't hide from what the future is going to bring."

"No, but you don't have to dwell on it, either." David chuckled. "Think about how many puppies you might want at one time."

Patty laughed. "That was absurd, although if

you're three years old I suppose it would make perfect sense. A puppy for each member of the family so you don't have to share. There you go.''

''That's five puppies you're talking about, which would mean a lot of puddles on the floor.''

''Five?'' Patty said.

''Well, yeah,'' David said, nodding. ''One for you, me, Tucker, Sarah Ann and Sophia. That's five any way you count it.''

''David, the five of us are not a family.''

''For now we are,'' he said, looking directly into her eyes. ''I can't project the future very well because I'm lacking too much data from the past. So I'm living in the present, the moment, enjoying today, and today we *are* functioning as a family. Yes?''

A lovely, comforting warmth suffused Patty, pushing aside the chill that the visions of the future had created within her. She smiled at David.

''Yes,'' she said. ''And I'll do a better job of remembering to enjoy the day I'm in. Thank you, David.''

He reached over and drew one thumb lightly over her lips, causing a shiver to course through her.

''You're welcome, Patty.''

The doorbell rang, announcing the arrival of Hannah and Ted, and bringing Tucker and Sarah Ann running down the hall with shrieks of excitement. The noise woke Sophia who wailed her displeasure at being wakened. After a rather chaotic ten minutes, David hobbled out the door on his crutches and managed to maneuver himself into Ted's vehicle.

''Off you go, Patty,'' Hannah said, as she attempted to soothe a still-crying Sophia she had scooped from her crib. "Now don't feel you have to hurry right home after your doctor's appointment. Stroll through a mall, indulge in a hot fudge sundae, go to a museum, something just for you while you have the chance."

"Oh, doesn't that sound tempting?" Patty said, smiling.

"Do it," her mother said. "Never turn down the opportunity to get away with no little ones in tow. This is the voice of experience talking here."

"Yes, ma'am," Patty laughed. "I always do what my mother tells me to."

"Your nose is going to grow, young lady," Hannah said. "Now, shoo."

"I'm gone." Patty kissed all three children good-bye, planted another kiss on her mother's cheek and started toward the door. "Have fun."

"Guaranteed," Hannah said.

Two hours later Patty sat on a bench inside a covered mall licking a three-scoop ice cream cone.

Delicious, she thought. One scoop of ice cream would have been enough, but she'd decided to go for the gusto. That, of course, had resulted in the momentous decision of what flavors to stack up on the sugar cone, plus say yes or no to sprinkles on top. The order that the chosen treats were placed on the cone was important, too, and…

Patty sighed, then continued to lick the ice cream before it dribbled down the cone and onto her hand.

Well, she'd exhausted the topic of the proper procedure to follow when purchasing an ice cream cone ad nauseam.

She was, she knew, skittering around the fact that her doctor had declared her to be fit as a fiddle—and had said she could resume intimate relations if she chose to do so. That had translated in her panicking mind into the fact that she was now free to make love with David Montgomery.

Patty popped the last bite of sugar cone into her mouth and stared into space, oblivious to the growing number of shoppers surrounding her.

She had readily agreed to take that step with David, even titled it a gift they would be giving each other for the duration of his stay at her house. Yep, she'd just jumped right in and said, "You betcha, big boy"...more or less. It had been very easy to act all womanly and sophisticated then, because she hadn't been in a position to do...it.

But now? Gracious. Now there were no excuses, nothing standing in their way, unless she wanted to grab hold of the age old "I have a headache" like a lifeline.

David was supposedly getting a smaller walking cast today, but if for some reason the doctor postponed that switch, she had a feeling that Mr. Montgomery wouldn't allow the bulky, cumbersome cast he'd started with to keep him from doing...it.

What happened next, Patty mused, was up to her. She could lie and tell David that the doctor hadn't released her yet. Or she could explain to David that she was very sorry but she'd changed her mind, just couldn't carry out her part of the bargain they'd made.

Patty narrowed her eyes.

Why was she entertaining such thoughts? Because she believed she shouldn't follow through on the plan since nice girls didn't have short-term affairs? Wanton women did, but not ones who placed motherhood and apple pie on the top of their list of priorities. No.

"Well, forget that nonsense," she said, getting to her feet.

"You're right," a woman said, causing Patty to jerk in surprise. "That gorgeous nightgown in the window isn't even close to being practical. I guess I'll stick to my flannel jammies."

Patty marched to where the woman stood.

"You want that nightie?" Patty said. "Then you should have it. Forget practical. Forget the fact that you'll probably get frostbite wearing it. Will it make you feel womanly, feminine? Yes, indeed it will, and we all deserve that once in a while."

"You're right," the woman said, nodding. "I'm going to buy it."

"Good for you."

"What about you?" the woman said. "Are you going to purchase a present for yourself, too?"

"No," Patty said. "I have a…a gift waiting for me at home and I intend to savor every lovely moment while it's mine."

"You have to give the gift back at some point?" the woman said, frowning.

"I don't qualify to keep it," Patty said, "which is a sad truth that I've accepted. Enjoy your beautiful nightie. 'Bye."

Patty frowned as she turned into her driveway and saw a vehicle she didn't recognize parked in front of the garage. It was a dark-green SUV with a temporary, new-vehicle certificate taped inside the back window. There was no sign of the car her parents had arrived in.

"What on earth is going on?" she said aloud, her heart racing with confusion edging quickly toward fear.

She ran across the yard, flung open the front door and entered the house. She stopped so quickly, she teetered, as she was met with a high-volume rendition of "The Bear Went Over the Mountain."

David was sitting on the sofa feeding Sophia a bottle while Tucker and Sarah Ann sat cross-legged in front of him on the floor singing along with him. It registered in some far corner of Patty's mind that David's injured leg was not propped straight out on the coffee table, but was bent at the knee like any normal leg.

She made her way forward slowly, arriving at the sofa just as the song ended terribly off-key.

"Hi, Mommy," Tucker said.

"Hi," she said. "David…"

"Hey, hi," he said, smiling at her. "Did you catch our singing act? We're ready for one of those TV shows where they discover talent and make people stars."

"David, where are my parents? Whose vehicle is in the driveway? What is going on here?"

David shrugged. "It's very simple. I got my cast switched to this spiffy new model that I can walk on without crutches and, bless their doctory hearts, wear right into the shower.

"Then your dad took me to the car dealership and between us we finagled a smokin' deal on that vehicle you see outside. The salesman called the insurance company. They agreed to send the check directly there and I drove that baby home.

"Upon arrival I assured your mother I could handle this brood, which prompted your father to invite her out to lunch. I fed the troops and we're having a sing-along for a few minutes before their naps. And there you have it."

Patty opened her mouth, closed it, then tried again.

"Oh," she said finally.

Tucker yawned.

"Okay," David said, getting to his feet as he popped the bottle out of Sophie's mouth. "Off to bed." He handed Sophia to a startled Patty. "Burp that one while I tuck the other two in. Let's march, march, march, Tucker and Sarah Ann. Show me how you can march."

Patty leveled Sophia up to her shoulder and patted her back absently as she watched, with a bemused expression on her face, the trio marching from the room, David moving exceptionally well in the new cast.

Sophia burped loudly, then lay her head down and closed her eyes. Patty made her way down the hall and placed the baby in her crib, hearing David telling Sarah Ann and Tucker they were to go right to sleep if they wanted Popsicles for their after-nap treat.

Patty fiddled with Sophia's blanket, smoothing it to exacting order, knowing she was stalling for time and rolling her eyes in self-disgust because she was.

This was it, she thought, turning from the crib. David was no doubt back in the living room now and would ask her how things had gone with her doctor's appointment. Oh, yes, this was most definitely the eleventh hour.

So why was she hesitating, not rushing to tell David her good news? Why was she questioning her decision yet again, darn it? This back and forth like a Ping-Pong ball stuff was driving her crazy.

"The gift," she whispered. "It's ours. David's and mine and we'll have it, just as we said. Yes. Oh, yes."

Patty left the nursery, went down the hall and entered the living room. David was stretched out on the sofa, facing away from her and she stood just inside the doorway, deciding to speak her piece from there, rather than look David straight in the eyes while she spoke.

"David," she said, then cringed when she heard the slight trembling in her voice. "David, I had a perfect checkup at the doctor and I am now allowed to... What I mean is, I can...if I want to...which I do, because we agreed to share our gift and it's not wrong, it's not. Oh, it's so difficult for me to say all this and... David, I want to make love with you. There. I'm shutting up now."

Patty clutched her hands on her stomach and waited for David to respond. And waited and waited...

A soft sound, something like a toy train running far in the distance, reached her and she inched her way toward the sofa to stand beside David. The toy-train noise was coming from his slightly parted lips as his chest rose and fell in a steady rhythm.

David Montgomery was fast asleep.

Chapter Nine

Patty sat down on the coffee table with a thud, staring at David, who continued to snooze. She narrowed her eyes as anger began to bubble within her, resulting in a flush staining her cheeks.

Oh-oh-oh, she was going to give this insensitive dolt a piece of her mind, she fumed, and at the top of her lungs, too, so he didn't miss one word of what she had to say.

Patty glanced quickly down the hallway.

Bad plan, she decided. If she hollered her head off, she'd wake all three of the children and that would never do. So, okay, she'd just have to get her point across in a normal tone of voice. Fine.

Patty leaned forward and poked David in the middle of his chest with one finger.

"You..."

"What? What?" he said, his eyes flying open.

"...are..."

"Patty?"

"...despicable." Patty lifted her chin and got to her feet. "I have spoken." She turned and walked in the direction of the kitchen.

"Hey, wait a minute," David said, struggling to sit up.

"No. And don't you dare wake those kids."

David stood and clomped his way after Patty, the walking cast leaving an impression in the carpeting. In the kitchen he found Patty sitting at the table with a glass of orange juice. He pulled out a chair and sat down opposite her.

"You're mad as hell at me, aren't you?" he said. "Could I have a clue, you know, just a hint as to why you're ready to shoot me dead as a post?"

"Oh, it's no big deal, David," she said, plunking the glass on the table. "So what if I went to the doctor today to find out if I could... To be informed as to whether or not I..."

"I stood there in the living room like an idiot, pouring my heart out to you, telling you how difficult it was for me to say what I was saying, telling you that I'd been released by the doctor and I...I wanted to share in our gift, I wanted to make love with you and...and...and...it was of so little importance to you to find out what the doctor said that you just flopped down on the sofa and went to sleep."

Tears filled Patty's eyes.

"You're...you're a...cad, David Montgomery. An insensitive, despicable cad." She sniffled. "Don't talk to me."

"Ah, Patty," he said, reaching across the table with one hand, which Patty smacked. He snatched it back. "Listen to me. Please? The entire time I was at my doctor's appointment I was wondering what was happening at *your* doctor's appointment. I daydreamed about holding you, kissing you, making sweet, sweet love to you for hours, sharing our gift. I was counting down the minutes until you'd tell me what your doctor said."

"Really?" Patty said dreamily, then blinked. "Oh."

"I didn't mean to fall asleep," he said, leaning toward her. "I should never have stretched out on the sofa because I knew I was exhausted. I only got snatches of sleep last night because my leg was itching so bad under that heavy plaster cast it felt like an army of ants was crawling around in there.

"I'm so very sorry that I conked out on you. I was waiting for you to come back down that hallway. Please, Patty, forgive me for hurting your feelings. I wouldn't do that for the world.

"I want you so much. I want to make love with you. I'd like to kick myself around the block for not hearing you say you want to make love with me, too. Don't take our gift away from us, Patty. I'm really very sorry."

David paused. "I didn't know anyone still said 'cad.' Insensitive, despicable cad? Whew. That's heavy stuff. But I deserve it. Do you want to call me any other names? Feel free. Go for it."

Patty stared at David for a long moment. A very long moment that caused a chill of dread to suffuse him as he stared at her staring at him.

Then Patty burst into laughter. She laughed so hard, she had to wrap her arms around her stomach and gasp for air.

"Is this what you do," David said tentatively, "before you slug someone you're really ticked off at?"

"Oh, my," Patty said, finally gaining control. "Hearing you repeat what I said made it sound so ridiculous. Insensitive, despicable cad? Cad? Oh, good grief. Don't get me started laughing again or I'll get the hiccups."

"Does this mean you're not mad anymore?" David said, raising his eyebrows.

"No, I'm not angry anymore, David," she said, shaking her head. "I was trying to be so womanly and sophisticated and telling you I wanted to make love with you was so out of character for me because I'm not womanly and sophisticated.

"It took every bit of courage I had to tell you what I did and then I saw that you were asleep and...I'm sorry you had a bad night with your leg. Why don't you go back to the sofa and nap while the children are asleep?"

"No way." David planted his hands flat on the table, leveled himself to his feet and started around the table. "I want you, and you want me, and we are going to make love that will be so special, so beautiful, it will defy description. Right now."

Patty's heart began to race as she watched David come closer and closer and...

He stopped next to her and extended one hand toward her, palm up.

"Yes?" he said, his voice very deep, very rumbly and very, very male.

Patty lifted one hand and placed it in David's, instantly feeling the warmth, the strength tempered with gentleness as she savored the sense of rightness about what she was about to do, what they would share. The gift.

She got to her feet and David dropped her hand to wrap his arms around her, nestling her to his rugged body as his mouth captured hers in a searing kiss that spoke of his want of her, matching the intensity of her desire for him.

He broke the kiss, and with his arm encircling her shoulders to keep her close to his side, they went down the hall to her bedroom, David closing the door behind them with a quiet click. He flipped back the blankets on the bed, then turned to Patty again.

"I've had two children," Patty said, her voice trembling slightly. "There are stretch marks and—"

"Shh," David said, framing her face in his hands. "You're so pretty, Patty. You said you aren't womanly or sophisticated. I don't know about sophisticated because I'm not sure how you're defining it, but I do know that you are very womanly, very feminine and lovely."

"Thank you," she whispered.

"No, I'm thanking you for allowing me to share our gift. I'm not getting high scores for remembering things right now, but I guarantee you that I will not forget what is about to take place between us. Ever."

But what about his wife? Marsha, Patty thought suddenly. David was assuming that the anger he'd felt radiating from her in his dream was directed toward him. But that might not be true. She might have been sad and angry because she knew she wasn't going to live long and would leave the man of her heart and the baby they had created together. When David's memory returned he would realize that and feel so guilty for making love with another woman and—

"Patty?" David said. "You're tensing up. Ah, please don't change your mind about this. We're living for the moment we're existing in. This is ours. We've agreed to give this to ourselves as a very precious gift."

Patty drew a steadying breath. "You're right. Nothing matters but this tick in time. Yes."

"Yes," he said, with a heartfelt sigh of relief.

He kissed her deeply, then they parted only long enough to shed their clothes and move onto the bed. Patty pushed aside the flash of embarrassment she felt about the stretch marks and her tummy that was not yet firm again after giving birth to Sophia.

Now, right now, she was beautiful, she thought, as she swept her gaze over David's naked body. And David was glorious, so perfectly proportioned with sculpted muscles and curly dark hair on his broad chest. His arousal announced his want of her. *Her.* She was a woman and she was about to make love with this magnificent man.

David kissed her as he skimmed one hand along the gentle slope of her hip. Then he shifted to take one of her full breasts into his mouth, laving the nipple with his tongue. Patty closed her eyes to savor every exquisite sensation sweeping throughout her, burning a path of heated desire as it went. He moved to the other breast as Patty's fingertips explored the bunching muscles of his back.

David's mouth melted over hers again and he

delved his tongue into the sweet darkness, finding her tongue, dueling, dancing, heightening their passion with every sensuous stroke. A soft sigh escaped from Patty's throat. A groan rumbled deep in David's chest.

"I'll protect you," he said finally, close to her lips, his voice gritty.

He left her for an eternity and she shivered with the need for him to return, to make her complete, to match so perfectly his manliness to her womanliness. He came to her, covering her body with his, then raising to catch his weight on his forearms to gaze directly into her eyes.

"I don't want to hurt you," he said. "Tell me if I'm hurting you."

"Shh. I want you. I do, David. Now."

He entered her slowly, tentatively, watching her face for any hint of discomfort, his arms quivering from the forced restraint.

Patty slid her hands to his lower back and raised her hips. David's control snapped and he thrust deep within her, bringing to her all that he was as a man.

"Oh...yes," she said softly. "Yes."

He began to move within her, slowly at first, then increasing the tempo to a pounding rhythm that Patty matched beat for beat.

It was ecstasy.

It was beautiful beyond description.

It was heat, coiling tighter and tighter, lifting them up and away to where they needed, wanted to go...together. Building. Hotter.

And then they were there.

They were flung into wondrous oblivion seconds

apart, whispering the name of the other, holding fast as rainbow colors surrounded them in the place where they had gone and nothing, no one, existed but the two of them. Waves of splendor rippled through them, one after the next, then finally stilled.

David collapsed against Patty, then mustered his last ounce of strength and rolled off her carefully. He tucked her close to his side, his lips resting on her moist forehead. Their bodies cooled and hearts returned to normal beats. Seconds became minutes, yet neither spoke.

"That was…" David said finally. "You are the most… Ah, Patty, I don't know what to say to you except our gift is rare and beautiful. Thank you."

"Oh, I thank you. I've never felt so… I don't have the words."

"We don't need words. We know."

"Yes." Patty paused. "I'd love to stay right here with you, but in case the kids wake up I'm going to take a quick shower."

"Mmm," David said, his lashes drifting down.

"Sleep," she said, smiling. "You're so tired."

"Mmm."

Patty slipped off the bed and drew the sheet up over David, who was already sound asleep. She gathered her clothes and went into the bathroom. After a warm shower, she dressed, then swiped her hand over the steamed-up mirror so she could see her reflection.

"Womanly," she said, leaning closer. "I'm going to go back into my mother mode now, but for a while, with David, I was beautiful and so womanly. Oh, David Montgomery, thank you so much for this gift."

* * *

David emerged from the bedroom freshly showered about five minutes after Tucker and Sarah Ann woke from their naps and came looking for a snack. Sophia was ready to eat, too, and the whole group went into the backyard to enjoy the perfect weather.

Sarah Ann and Tucker sat on the glider of the swing set and ate Popsicles while Patty settled onto a lawn chair to feed Sophia. David sat in the other lawn chair next to them.

"As corny as it might be," he said, "I'm going to comment on the weather. What a great day."

"Yes, it is," Patty said. "It's a day to remember."

She turned her head to look at David to discover he was smiling directly at her.

"Oh, yes, ma'am," he said. "I certainly intend to remember this day." He chuckled. "I realize, as I said before, that I have a lousy reputation in the memory department, but today is a keeper…guaranteed."

"That's nice," Patty said, matching his smile.

"Mommy," Tucker yelled. "We're done with our Popsicles."

"Bring your sticks up here and put them in the trash can," Patty said.

Tucker and Sarah Ann ran to the patio and dropped their sticky sticks in the trash can as they'd been told.

"Will you push us on the swings, Mommy?" Tucker asked. "I want to go all the way to the sky."

"I can't right now, Tucker," Patty said. "I'm feeding Sophia."

"You *always* feed Sophia," Tucker said, frowning. "She just eats and eats and sleeps and sleeps, and gets stinky diapers all the time."

Patty laughed. "Which is exactly what you did when you were this little, toughy Tucker."

"You got stinky diapers," Sarah Ann said in a singsong voice.

"Did not," Tucker said.

"Did too," Sarah Ann said. "Your mommy just said you did. So there."

"And *your* daddy," David said, "is saying that you did the same thing, Sarah Ann. In fact, I remember taking you to the park and I ran out of diapers. You really, I mean really, needed to have a fresh one and you yelled your head off all the way home. You nearly broke my ears."

Sarah Ann covered her mouth with her hands and giggled in charming little-girl fashion.

"I'll push you two on the swings," David said, levering himself up.

"Yippee," Tucker said, and the pair ran back toward the swings.

"I assume you made that story up about Sarah Ann's diaper," Patty said quietly.

"No, I didn't," David said, looking down at her. "That actually happened and I can see it in my mind as clear as a bell. There must have been a park close to where we lived because I had Sarah Ann in a rather old-fashion-style buggy, a pram, or whatever." He nodded. "People were staring at us as I pushed the thing out of the park because she was wailing at full volume."

"Were you…were you alone?"

"Yes. It was just me and Sarah Ann, and I was annoyed at myself for not putting enough diapers in the bag."

"You packed the diaper bag for the outing?" Patty asked.

David nodded slowly. "I'm sure I did, but I can't see the house where we came from and were headed back to. Well, something is better than nothing as far as my memory goes, I guess, but it isn't exactly a momentous thing. My daughter needed her diaper changed and was not a happy camper because that demand was not being tended to immediately. Wow. Stop the presses."

"Don't belittle it, David," Patty said. "Everything you remember is important because it represents your memory returning."

"Daddy," Sarah Ann yelled. "We're ready to swing to the sky."

"Yes, your highnessship," David said, laughing as he made his way across the yard.

And everything that David remembered, Patty thought, brought him one step closer to recovering from the amnesia and being ready to return home with his daughter. Well, yes, of course, she knew that. She would miss David Montgomery when he left. She would miss him very, very much.

David suggested that they all go out for pizza to celebrate the fact that he could now drive and even had a vehicle large enough to cart them all.

At six o'clock that evening they were in a noisy, crowded pizza restaurant, Sophia nestled in her carrier on top of the table next to the wall. Tucker was seated by Patty across from David and Sarah Ann. The pizza was delicious.

"You know, David," Patty said, between bites.

"You might give some thought to calling the Fuzzy Bunny and letting them know Sarah Ann will be returning in the future. I haven't spoken to anyone there since the night I stayed late because you hadn't arrived on time.

"They haven't phoned me so I assumed they figure you were just held up in traffic. But you don't want to lose Sarah Ann's spot after the fees you've paid run out. I've already made arrangements to enroll Tucker in January. There's a waiting list to get into the Fuzzy Bunny."

"Okay," David said, nodding. "I'll call them tomorrow. I'll just say I'm laid up at home and Sarah Ann is with me there. If I need to pay more tuition to keep her space reserved, I'll have to go to my house and try to figure out where my checkbook is."

"Can I have more soda?" Tucker said.

"*May* I have more soda," Patty said, then poured two inches into his glass. "David and I were talking about the Fuzzy Bunny, Tucker. Won't it be super when you and Sarah Ann are going there together again?"

"No," Tucker said. "I don't want to go without you, Mommy. Never ever."

"Just checking," Patty said under her breath.

A couple in their sixties stopped at the end of the table, and Patty and David looked up at them questioningly.

"We're sorry to disturb you," the woman said, smiling, "but my husband and I just wanted to say what a lovely family you are. Our children and grandchildren live so far away and we just soaked up the sound of your little ones' laughter.

"You're both so patient with them, too. In these stressful times we see so many parents who are obviously at the end of their tether when it comes to dealing with their children. It just warmed our hearts to see a mother and father who are relaxed and happy and thoroughly enjoying their children the way they should."

"Oh, but—" Patty started.

"Thank you," David interrupted. "We appreciate your taking the time to tell us that. We think our munchkins are pretty special. Don't we, Patty?"

"Yes, we do," she said.

"We'll let you get back to your pizza," the woman said. "Goodbye."

"Goodbye," David said, beaming. "And thanks again."

As the couple moved away, Patty looked quickly at Tucker and Sarah Ann and saw that they were finished eating and were coloring the paper placemats that had been provided for the kids, along with a basket of crayons. She leaned forward slightly.

"Why did you allow those people to believe we are a family?" she said. "That wasn't honest, David."

He shrugged. "It was a lot easier than explaining the complicated truth, for crying out loud. We're sitting here functioning as a family, so what the heck? No harm was done."

"You're right, I suppose." Patty laughed. "Well, pat us on the back for being patient parents with our brood."

"We *are* good parents," David said, suddenly serious.

"Yes," Patty said, her smile disappearing. "Being a mother is a role I perform very well. It makes up for the fact that I fall short as a... Never mind. Why don't you eat that last slice of pizza?"

"Fall short as a what?" David said. "Not as a woman, that's for sure. I could swear to that under oath."

"David, hush. Someone will hear you."

"In this noisy place? Won't happen. That only leaves the role of a wife as far as I can tell. What makes you believe that you fall short, to quote, as a—"

"Shh. This isn't the time or the place to discuss this. In fact, I don't wish to discuss it at any time or in any place." Patty shifted her gaze to Tucker and Sarah Ann. "Oh, you both are coloring inside the lines so nicely. We'll take those placemats home and put them on the refrigerator."

Well, damn, David thought. Even after what they'd shared, the incredibly beautiful lovemaking they'd engaged in, Patty was still buttoned up about what had happened to her marriage to Peter the jerk.

She continually made it sound as though it was *her* fault the sleazeball had deserted his family for another woman. That was nuts, totally insane. Any man lucky enough to have Patty Clark as his wife and the mother of his children should be saying a prayer of thanks every day of his life.

Would Patty ever trust him enough to pour out her heart to him, share her pain, explain what had happened with her and Peter? God, he hoped so. Why it meant so much to him, he didn't know. But it did. It really did.

"Tucker, Sarah Ann, finish coloring your pictures," Patty said, "because Sophia is going to start fussing for a bottle any minute now. Not only that, there are people waiting for this table and we're all done being piggies with our pizza."

"We're not piggies," Sarah Ann said, laughing. "We're bears, remember? My daddy said me and Tucker are baby bears."

"Oh, let's not start that again," Patty said, rolling her eyes heavenward.

Sophia began to cry and David reached over and wiggled her foot.

"What's the matter, Goldilocks?" he said. "Ready for some chow?"

"Put the crayons back in the basket," Patty said.

"Not yet, Mommy," Tucker said.

"Hey," David said. "Do it, sport, then you and Sarah Ann grab your placemats and we're out of here. Those are direct orders from your daddy bear and mama bear."

"'Kay," Tucker said, putting his crayon in the basket.

"I thought we agreed not to play the bear game anymore, David," Patty said, frowning as she slid out of the booth.

"No, you expressed your opinion about it, but I don't recall agreeing with you." David got to his feet, then leaned over and picked up Sophia's carrier. "But to keep you smiling, I won't do it again after tonight. How's that?"

"Fine. Thank you."

"*After* tonight," David said, grinning at her. He switched his attention to Tucker and Sarah Ann.

"Goldilocks is hungry, so baby bear Tucker and baby bear Sarah Ann, haul yourselves out of that booth. It's time to hit the road with your daddy bear and mama bear. Yep, it's time to go home."

Chapter Ten

That night David insisted that he would now sleep on the sofa since he no longer wore the bulky cast, nor did he have to elevate his leg. It was time, he declared, that Patty got a decent night's sleep in her own bed.

Patty opened her mouth to begin a debate on the subject, but when David narrowed his eyes and crossed his arms over his chest, she mentally threw up her hands in defeat. She knew that I'm-not-budging-on-this-one body language of his and there was no sense in wasting time and energy engaging in an argument she wouldn't win.

But before David took up residence on the sofa, he and Patty made sweet, slow love in her bed, once more soaring into wondrous oblivion as they whispered the name of the other.

The next day David watched over Sarah Ann, Tucker and Sophia while Patty shopped for groceries, David insisting that she use some of the fairly large amount of money he'd discovered in his wallet.

The day after that, which was Wednesday, they went shopping for new tennis shoes for Tucker and Sarah Ann with David pushing Sophia's stroller through the crowded mall. They went into a pet shop to allow the three-year-olds to watch the fish in a huge aquarium, then ended the outing with ice cream cones eaten in an old-fashioned-style ice cream parlor.

On Thursday Patty packed a picnic lunch in a wicker basket and they went to the park, all three children falling asleep on the way home.

And every night Patty and David made love, shared their gift, before he settled in on the sofa.

Friday evening they were invited to dinner at Patty's parents' house and a good time was had by all. Ted asked David if he'd be interested in playing some golf once his leg was healed, and after a long and concentrated moment, David said he didn't know if he was a fan of the sport.

"I don't have a clue, Ted," he said.

"Maybe you've never played," Ted said. "That would be great because it would mean there's a chance you're even more inept at hitting that devilish little white ball than Ryan and I are. We have a fortune of golf balls sitting in the bottom of the water traps on the course. I should take up snorkeling and retrieve those things."

During the evening Patty was the recipient of a multitude of what appeared to her to be rather smug smiles produced by her mother. When Patty cornered

Hannah in the kitchen and asked her what her problem was, Hannah smiled once again and patted her daughter on the cheek.

"I know what I know," was all that Hannah would say.

They returned to Patty's in time to put all three children to bed, enjoyed two family sitcoms on television, then followed their custom of watching the ten-o'clock news. Halfway through the broadcast, the anchorwoman announced that after the commercial break they would be showing another segment of the series about dangerous roads in California.

"I hope this series is resulting in people driving more slowly in the areas they're showing," Patty said, "and some good is coming from the depressing stories they're telling of people who have been killed."

David lifted one shoulder in a shrug. "It will probably make drivers more alert for a while, but before long they'll go back to the way they were. That's human nature, I guess, which is too bad because this station has done an excellent job gathering data and presenting the information."

Patty nodded, then the commercials ended and the anchorwoman was once more smiling at them.

"Our series on dangerous roads continues," she said. "And tonight we are focusing on a stretch of highway located north of San Francisco. As you can see from the film the road is narrow, has sharp turns and steep drop-offs. Many people refer to this section as Dark Death Road as there are no homes close enough to cast even the faintest light on the multitude of tight curves. The number of accidents..."

As the woman went on, a sharp pain sliced through David's head for a moment, causing his breath to catch. In the next instant he felt as though he'd been punched in the solar plexus and sweat dotted his brow.

Visions tumbled through his mind, one after the other, vivid and stark and real. A woman with long, blond hair who shoved a crying Sarah Ann at David, then hurried out of a doorway, slamming the door behind her.

A photograph in a newspaper of a crushed car retrieved from the bottom of a deep ravine. Pictures in the same paper showing a man and a woman in candid photos and identifying them as the people who had been killed in the accident.

A cemetery on a gloomy, rainy day with a wild wind whipping the rain into a frenzy, drenching David as he stood staring at the casket waiting to be lowered into the ground.

"My God," David said, his voice raspy. "Oh, my God."

"David?" Patty said anxiously. "What is it? What's wrong? You're as pale as a ghost and your hands are trembling and... Are you ill? David?"

"My...wife...Marsha..." he said, turning his head slowly to meet Patty's frightened gaze. "She was killed on that road. The car went over the side and... She was leaving me and Sarah Ann to go off with her lover. She didn't want to be a wife and mother anymore. She found it suffocating, boring.

"She was a paralegal our firm hired temporarily for a big case I was working on," David continued, speaking in a monotone. "She was beautiful, vivacious, almost ten years younger than me, and razzed me all the time about how I was becoming a stodgy old man who did nothing but work. I was captivated by her, by her zest for life, her ability to turn every day into an adventure centered on people and fun.

"We started dating and I was swept into her world of nightclubs, drinking, dancing, other people who lived as though there was no tomorrow. It was so different from anything I had ever known, *she* was so different from the women I had dated in the past, and I was grateful she had come into my life. I was convinced she was the best thing that had ever happened to me, because I really was doing nothing but work."

David drew a shuddering breath.

"I was so very certain that I had found my life's partner, my soul mate, and I asked her to marry me. She agreed and we continued our lifestyle of going out almost every night to the clubs where she seemed to know everyone who came through the door. If I had to work late, I'd meet her at a club where she'd already been for several hours. Then…"

"Then?" Patty whispered, her gaze riveted on David as her heart raced.

"Marsha got pregnant. She was furious, said she had no intention of having a baby, being tied down at home buried in diapers and bottles, and I begged her to have the baby, told her I'd hire all the help she needed and that I wanted to be a father. She refused, but then discovered she was further along than she thought and it was too late to terminate the pregnancy. Three nights after she gave birth to Sarah Ann, she went dancing and I stayed home with our newborn daughter."

"Oh, David," Patty said, shaking her head.

"I hired a nurse to tend to Sarah Ann," he went on, pain echoing in his voice and visible on his face. "I rarely saw Marsha because she went out every night and I took over Sarah Ann's care when I came home from work. We actually lived that way for months. I was devoted to the baby, loved her so much.

"But I couldn't face the fact that I'd made such a terrible mistake by marrying Marsha. Talk about faulty judgment. I had seen her as I wanted her to be, not as she really was. She was selfish, self-centered, and immature. I knew I must never again trust myself in regard to knowing the true nature of a woman.

"Over a year ago Marsha said she was filing for divorce, was leaving the area with her lover and would give me full custody of Sarah Ann. She'd had her fill of being a wife and mother. The night she left it was raining. She and that man had been drinking, and he miscalculated a turn on Dark Death Road and drove over the edge. They were both killed."

"Dear heaven," Patty said, feeling the color drain from her face.

"I realized at Marsha's funeral," David said, swiping his thumb over his moist forehead, "that I wasn't mourning her. Our marriage had been over for months, she was a stranger to me, someone I had chosen to spend my future with who wasn't even close to being who I had believed her to be. The only good thing that came from that marriage was Sarah Ann."

"David, you don't have to talk about this anymore," Patty said, hearing the trembling in her voice.

"Your memory has returned because of what you saw on television about that road, but it is obviously very painful for you to relive all of what you're telling me."

"There isn't that much more to say," he said, sounding exhausted. "I concentrated on Sarah Ann, wanted to be the best father I could be, but I had such a heavy workload and I traveled a great deal for the firm as well because the other partners were getting up in years.

"I visited Ventura and liked what I saw. I made the decision to move here, start fresh with my daughter and open my own firm where I could control the number of hours I worked. I wouldn't make as much money, I knew, but I had plenty of cash because I had sold my partnership to my replacement, plus I'd spent so many years before I married Marsha being too busy to enjoy the fruits of my labor.

"The house..." David nodded. "I bought the house where you went to get Sarah Ann's clothes. I know where it is and what it looks like. I was finishing getting settled, then planned to start looking for office space somewhere. I figured I could hire a part-time housekeeper to keep the place in order and prepare our dinner.

"Well, there you have it," he said, an edge to his voice. "The exciting tale of how I ended up in Ventura, California. Older, but much wiser. I have a major, big-time flaw in regard to women. I see what I want to see, not what is truly there. I'm a top-notch attorney, I'll give myself that. But in the man-and-woman relationship arena? I'm a dud, a complete failure."

So am I, Patty thought miserably.

David dragged both hands down his face.

"Man, I'm tired," he said. "I feel as though I just ran in a marathon or something. Getting your memory back really takes it out of a person, I guess. Or maybe it's only draining as hell when the remembered reality isn't exactly sunshine and roses." He paused. "Ah, Patty, I shouldn't have dumped the whole story on you. That wasn't fair and I'm sorry."

"Don't say that, David," Patty said, placing one hand on his knee. "You didn't dump on me. You shared, and I listened to every word because I care about you, want to know who you are and where life took you before we met." She paused. "Do you have family? Parents? Brothers? Sisters?"

"No. My folks were both only children. I was a late-in-life surprise and my parents died within six months of each other when I was in law school. My entire family consists of Sarah Ann."

"That's not true," Patty said, removing her hand from his knee. "Technically it is, but a family consists of people who care about each other. The Sharpes are considered part of the MacAllister family but we're not really related.

"My father and Ryan MacAllister were partners on the police force for many years. Then when Ryan quit they remained close. I forget at times that Robert and Margaret MacAllister are not really my grandparents and that people I view as aunts, uncles, cousins are not blood relatives.

"You and Sarah Ann aren't alone. You have me, Tucker, Sophia, and you're being welcomed into the MacAllister clan, too. I hate the thought that you feel you're without family support because that isn't true.''

"Thank you, that's very nice," David sighed. "I'll have to give that some thought, but at the moment I'm on emotional overload. So many memories, so much to deal with all at once."

"You're exhausted, David. You need to go to bed and get some sleep."

David managed to produce a small smile. "You're sitting on my bed."

"So I am," Patty said, rising. "I'll be very quick in the bathroom so you can get in there."

"No, I think I'll just sit here a while and try to unwind. I'm so wired I'll never be able to sleep. I'll use the bathroom in the hall later. You go on to bed."

"You're not...you're not coming to bed with me?"

David took one of Patty's hands in his. "Not tonight. Okay? I really need some time to sift and sort through everything that is tumbling through my mind. Do you understand?"

"Of course. Sure. Good night, David. I guess congratulations are in order for regaining your memory. Your amnesia ordeal is over. Sleep well."

"Good night," David said quietly, then watched as Patty hurried from the room and disappeared from view.

He leaned his head on the top of the sofa and stared at the ceiling, so thoroughly drained that he felt he wouldn't be able to move even if the house was on fire.

He raised his head again slowly and narrowed his eyes as he swept his gaze over the familiar room.

It was as though, he thought, there was another

entity here now, someone who hadn't been part of this household before, hadn't interacted with the three children, hadn't made exquisite love with Patty, hadn't basked in the warmth and laughter within these walls.

And that shadowy someone was him. The part of him that had been missing had been found, was here, demanding attention and space, refusing to be ignored. He was whole again. The nightmare of the amnesia was over, yet that meant he had to face who he truly was, all of him, complete with an overwhelming flaw.

He did not possess the ability to see women as they truly were, viewing them instead as what he wanted them to be.

David looked toward the hallway where Patty had gone.

Oh, but that didn't include Patty Sharpe Clark, he thought, with an edge of franticness. She was exactly who she presented herself to be. Honest, open and real, a dedicated mother, a passionate woman. She didn't have an agenda that would make her less than what he believed her to be. Not Patty.

Why not Patty? a little voice niggled in his mind. Why should his judgment about her be any better than it had been about Marsha? Yes, Patty had a secret she hadn't shared with him that centered somehow on her role of wife to Peter. What other secrets did she harbor? What was he failing to comprehend about her, not seeing as the truth that it was as he filled his mind—and his heart—with who he believed her to be?

"Oh, God," David said, shaking his head.

He was driving himself crazy, he thought. He had to shut off his mind, get some rejuvenating sleep, face his reality in the light of the new day. He couldn't deal with the turmoil in his mind anymore tonight. Not tonight.

David levered himself to his feet and made his way down the hall to the bathroom to prepare for bed, feeling as though a crushing weight was pressing painfully against him, making it difficult to place one foot in front of the other.

Patty lay in bed, one hand splayed on the empty space where David was supposed to be.

So, she thought, struggling against threatening tears, this was it. The end. David had regained his memory and could return to his home with Sarah Ann, knowing where everything was that he'd un-packed and put away, aware of any special rituals he took part in with his daughter that might be different from what she was participating in here, remembering all the little things he shared with Sarah Ann.

And this was the end of the gift.

Patty sniffled.

Good grief, she was feeling so sorry for herself, she thought with a flash of disgust. She was centering on the fact that David was going to leave and take his daughter with him. He would no longer live under her roof, take an active part in outings and fun-filled meals, stories at bedtime for sleepy three-year-olds, bathing and feeding Sophia.

And he would not make love to her in this bed, hold her so close after sharing the intimate act, then kiss her deeply before heading for his spot on the sofa. He would not be here to make her feel so womanly and feminine, allow her to separate, as they shared their gift, the woman from the mother...just for a little while.

It was over.

But, dear heaven, she was being so selfish. She should be focusing on how she might be sympathetic and supportive as David dealt with the harsh truths of his disaster of a marriage to Marsha that had ultimately resulted in the violent death of his unfaithful wife.

Wife. She had been a pseudo-wife to David for this brief interlude they'd had together. They'd been a family, the five of them, doing all the things together that families engaged in. In the role of wife-for-the-moment, the mama bear, she should be standing ready to see the husband, the father bear, through this trying and difficult time he was facing.

But was she doing that? No, not Patty Sharpe Clark. She was, instead, wallowing in self-pity because her fantasy world was about to return to the reality that she was a single mother raising two young children. Alone. Which was par for the course, she supposed, because she had failed Peter.

And tonight she had failed David.

David was convinced that he had a major flaw—the inability to see women as they really were instead of what he believed them to be. It was obvious from what he had related that Marsha had not shown her true colors until she had gotten pregnant.

David shouldn't blame himself for choosing a vivacious, outgoing woman to be his wife, someone who added excitement and fun to his existence.

There was no way he could have known how self-centered and selfish Marsha was because that part of her hadn't surfaced until she was carrying his child. David was standing in harsh judgment of himself, which he didn't deserve.

The same would hold true if history had been different. If David Montgomery had met, fallen in love with and married her, Patty Clark, in the distant past, he would have learned through no fault of his own that she was not capable of meeting his needs in the role of his wife.

That glaring truth had been very evident again tonight as she'd left him alone to deal with his demons and retreated to her bedroom where she could sniffle into her pillow and think only of herself and what she would no longer have when David returned home.

Oh, Patty, go to sleep, she ordered herself. She didn't feel like spending any more time in her own company. Tomorrow morning she would once again mesh the woman with the mother, focusing on Tucker and Sophia, ignoring the woman within her until she was eclipsed by the mother who was very, very good at what she did. She was a wonderful mother and she would hold fast to that truth like a lifeline.

Patty pulled her hand slowly back from where it was splayed on David's space in the bed, then turned over and faced the other way. She centered her thoughts on what she would do in the light of the new day to bring smiles to the faces of her children, ignoring the tears that slid down her cheeks.

At breakfast the next morning Patty kept up a nearly non-stop chatter directed at the children about what a nice sunny day it was, and how if they finished their eggs they could watch an hour of Saturday cartoons, then informing a babbling Sophia that she was getting to be such a big girl, just growing so fast, and on and on.

When Tucker and Sarah Ann had cleared their plates, Patty found the proper television channel for them, then placed Sophia in her carrier next to the pair on the floor.

"There you go," Patty said brightly. "One hour of cartoons, no more, then I'll get you dressed. Okay? Enjoy."

She zoomed back into the kitchen, throwing a glance in David's direction where he still sat at the table. He had his elbows propped on the placemat and his coffee mug nestled in his hands as he watched her begin to clean the kitchen.

"You're chipper this morning," he finally said quietly.

"It's Saturday," Patty said, concentrating on wiping off a counter that was already sparkling clean. "It's silly when you realize that I'm home every day anyway, but there's something different about Saturdays, a sense of freedom and fun, chores put on hold so there's more time to be with my children." She attempted a laugh that didn't quite materialize. "I told you it was silly."

"Patty, could you come sit down over here? Please?"

"Well, I'd really like to get this kitchen shipshape while the kids are occupied with their rationed cartoon time and—"

"Please?"

Patty stilled, sighed, then rinsed out the cloth and hung it over the faucet. She walked slowly to the table and sat opposite David, immediately beginning to trace the outline of the fire truck on Tucker's placemat with one fingertip.

"Patty," David said, "look at me. I'm not in the mood to play second fiddle to a picture of a fire truck."

Patty clutched her hands in her lap and met David's frowning gaze.

"Yes?" she said, her voice not quite steady.

"We both know," he said, fatigue evident on his face and in his voice, "that there is no longer any reason for me to stay here in your home. We were waiting for my memory to return and it has. It's time for me and Sarah Ann to leave."

"But you don't have the housekeeper you spoke of last night," Patty said, an edge to her voice. "You can't possibly prepare proper meals for Sarah Ann because you're a terrible cook. Wouldn't it be best for Sarah Ann if you interviewed women for the position of the part-time housekeeper while you're still here? It would make the transition so much easier for your daughter, David."

"I—"

"For that month or so that you were getting settled and brought Sarah Ann to the Fuzzy Bunny," Patty rushed on, "what did you do about dinner after you picked her up?"

David shrugged. "I took her to a family restaurant or a fast-food place, or had take-out delivered to the house. I made her toast, cereal, fruit for breakfast. A temporary diet of dinners that don't contain all the major food groups or whatever isn't going to do permanent damage to a healthy little kid.''

''No, but it isn't necessary for her to eat meals like that because you can stay right here until you find the perfect housekeeper to prepare your dinners and keep your home spick-and-span.''

David narrowed his eyes. ''Why are you doing this? Why are you pushing for us to stay when we both know the agreement was that I would leave when my memory came out of mothballs?''

''Because it would be best for Sarah Ann,'' Patty said, leaning forward slightly.

''Oh? Or maybe there's more to it than that,'' he said, his voice sharp. ''Like, oh, let's see here. My entertaining the kids while you cook dinner without little fingers in the way? Or my willingness to give Sophia her bottle while riding herd on the others so you could have some private time at the mall or wherever? And there's my helping with bedtime stories, and hauling groceries and pitching in a buck or two to pay my share.''

Patty felt the color drain from her face. ''What are you saying?''

''Wait, wait,'' David said. ''I'm not finished with my list. Let us not forget, Ms. Clark, that dynamite sex is very much in this mix. Night after night of good, ol' lusty sex. My point is, Patty, that I can't help wondering if you want us to stay on here now for reasons other than it being best for Sarah Ann.''

''You don't mean that,'' Patty said, shaking her head. ''You can't believe I'm using you to make my life easier with the children and to satisfy my sexual urges and...

"David, you're obviously tired, and I'm assuming you didn't sleep well last night because you had so much to deal with, so many memories to deal with. Let's just forget this nasty conversation took place, shall we? You can scoot into my bedroom and take a nap."

"You're treating me like a child again," David said, none too quietly. He glanced quickly at the kitchen doorway, then lowered his volume when he spoke again. "You're really in your mother mode this morning, huh? I thought you'd become comfortable as a woman around me. Obviously I was wrong. But that should come as no surprise to me because I have a heavy-duty history of being wrong about what I believe about a woman."

Patty's eyes widened. "Is *that* what this is all about? You're suddenly looking at me through the eyes of the man who saw what he wanted to see in Marsha? You're doing that to *me* after all we've shared? Our gift, our special and beautiful gift? Oh, David, don't do this.

"I'm me—Patty," she went on, splaying one hand on her breasts. "How can you question my motives like this? What's next? You wonder if I'm trying to snag you as my next husband because I like the size of your bank account?

"I mean, hey, I've made it clear that I don't want to return to teaching or leave my children in day care. What better way to be able to stay home than to latch on to a money machine, a guy with deep pockets? Is that scenario on your mind, too, David?"

David didn't speak. His face was suddenly void of any readable expression as he stared at Patty.

"David?" Patty whispered. "You can't believe that. Not that or any of the other hateful things you said. Oh, please, David, you know who and what I am. You do."

"No," he said, his voice gritty with emotion. "I know who I *want* you to be, who I've convinced myself that you are. But the truth of the matter, Patty? Now that I know who *I* am, I have to face the truth, the fact that I really don't know you at all."

Chapter Eleven

Patty had to tell herself to breathe, to inhale, then exhale, and to ignore the searing pain from what David had said that was slicing through her.

Do not cry, she ordered herself. She would not allow this man to shred her pride as well as her...as well as her heart. No, forget that. Her heart wasn't involved in this, not one iota. But then again, oh, dear heaven, she was going to fall apart, just dissolve into a weeping mess.

"I..." she said, pushing herself to her feet. "I'd better go check on the children. Yes. I need to do that."

Before Patty could escape from the kitchen and from David, Tucker came running into the room.

"Mommy, Sarah Ann threw up all over Sophia and the floor and it's really yucky and gross."

"What?" Patty said, staring at him with wide eyes. "Oh, good heavens."

Patty ran from the room with David hobbling right behind her and found the scene in front of the television in the living room exactly as Tucker had described it. With the arrival of the adults, Sarah Ann burst into tears. Patty dropped to her knees beside her.

"It's all right, sweetie," she said, placing one hand on Sarah Ann's forehead. "You've got a little tummy bug, that's all."

"She was fine at breakfast," David said.

"This is how quickly kids can get sick," Patty said, not looking up at him. "Come on, Sarah Ann, let's get you into a warm tub to clean you up, then tuck you back into bed."

"What do you want *me* to do?" David said.

Patty got to her feet and spun around to face him.

"Oh, that's right," she said, a definite edge to her voice. "One of the reasons I've urged you to stay here is to be available to help me with the children. Well, fine. Get the baby's bathtub and some clean clothes for her and tend to her in the kitchen. Or you can give Sarah Ann her bath."

"No," Sarah Ann said, sniffling. "I want you, Patty. My tummy hurts. It does."

"Daddy will take care of you, Sarah Ann," David said.

"No," she said. "I want my mommy. I want Patty."

"But..." David said.

"This isn't the time to argue the point," Patty said. "Come on, Sarah Ann. David, give Sophia a bath. Tucker, stay put in front of the television for now, but stay away from where Sarah Ann was sick, sweet-heart.''

"'Kay,'' Tucker said, plunking back down on the floor.

"Whatever,'' David said, starting across the room. "I'll get Sophia's bathtub. But I'm perfectly capable of taking care of my own daughter and—''

"No, no, no,'' Sarah Ann said, then fresh tears started.

Close to an hour later, David sank onto the sofa with a freshly bathed and dressed Sophia in his arms. He poked a bottle in her mouth and she ate with gusto as she stared at him.

"You're as good as new,'' he said, looking at the baby. "The kitchen is a disaster, but it will have to wait for now. You're a trooper, Sophia. I don't think I would have been as pleasant as you if a kid threw up breakfast on me. You're a sweet girl and…and I'm going to miss you, munchkin.''

Tucker turned from where he was still watching cartoons while sitting on the floor.

"How comes you're going to miss Sophia?'' he said. "She can't go on a trip or something without all of us 'cause she doesn't even know how to walk or anything like that. She has to stay right here, so you don't have to miss her, David.''

"Tucker,'' he said quietly, "you have to remember that Sarah Ann and I don't really live here. We've just been visiting until…until my leg was a bit better, which it is. It's time Sarah Ann and I went to our own house to sleep.''

Tucker jumped to his feet and came to where David

was sitting, flinging himself across one of David's thighs.

"I don't want you to leave," Tucker said. "Your leg isn't all better 'cause you still gots that thing on it. You should stay here longer, David. Sarah Ann is my bestis friend and we have fun and stuff. And you have fun 'cause you laugh a lot. You like it here, don't you? Sure." His bottom lip began to tremble. "I don't want you to go."

"Oh, man," David said. "Tucker, don't cry. Okay, buddy? Come on, show me a big smile."

Tucker levered himself upward and folded his arms over his little chest.

"No," he said, tears filling his eyes. "I won't smile for you ever again, ever. I want my mommy."

Tucker ran down the hall, and David's shoulders slumped. He pulled the bottle from Sophia's mouth, set it on the end table, then lifted her to his shoulder where he patted her gently on the back. Sophia began to fuss.

"You're unhappy, too?" he said, lowering her again and offering the bottle which she refused to accept. "I'm batting a thousand here. Shh. Don't cry. That's it. Close your eyes. Nappy time. That's my girl. Shh."

Sophia's eyes drifted closed.

That's my girl? David mentally repeated. No, Sophia wasn't his. She belonged to Patty, just as Tucker did. And at the moment his own daughter preferred Patty over him.

Patty.

God, he'd ripped into her, couldn't seem to stop the hateful words that had poured out of his mouth, one after another. He'd ignored the pain he'd seen on her face, in her beautiful dark eyes, and just kept flinging accusations at her.

All of which could very well be true.

All of which could very well be false.

He didn't know what the truth was, he thought miserably, and that was his flaw, the thing he had to protect himself against. Each cutting word he'd said to Patty was a brick in the wall he was building around his heart to keep it safe from her, to be certain she didn't stake a claim on it.

But, oh, God, he'd hurt her so badly. What kind of a man did something like that? She'd opened her home to him and his daughter, strangers really, who needed help through a crisis. She'd treated Sarah Ann with loving care, as though she were her own daughter and she'd given the very essence of herself to him in the form of the gift, their incredibly wondrous lovemaking.

But why had Patty done all those things? David thought. Because she was the sweet, honest, caring woman she presented herself to be, or because she was setting him up to achieve the goals of her own selfish agenda? He didn't know what the answer to that question was, didn't possess the ability to tell fact from fiction in regard to who a woman really was.

And so he had to go, leave this home and Tucker and Sophia. Leave Patty. He had to do that to be assured that he didn't make another major mistake in his life the way he had when he'd believed in Marsha. He had no choice in the matter. None. Ah, hell, what a mess.

David was pulled from his tormenting thoughts by

Patty coming into the living room carrying Tucker, who had his arms wrapped around her neck and his face buried in her shoulder.

"Was it really necessary, David," Patty said tightly, "to announce that you're leaving and taking Sarah Ann with you while we're in the midst of an upset around here? Your timing leaves a lot to be desired, mister."

"I'm sorry," David said, struggling himself to his feet. "You're right, and I apologize. Hey, Tucker, come on, buddy, we're still friends, aren't we?"

"No," came the muffled reply.

"Dandy," David said. "I'll go put Sophia in her crib. How's Sarah Ann?"

"She's sleeping," Patty said, rubbing Tucker's back in a circular motion. "She has a slight temperature and I gave her some baby aspirin. I'll have a better idea of what is going on with her when she wakes up. Tucker, honey, I have to scrub the carpet by the television so you sit on the sofa for now."

"No," Tucker mumbled.

"I'll clean the carpet," David said, "after I put Sophia down."

"Fine," Patty said coolly, sinking onto a chair with Tucker. "That's part of the reason I've kept you around. Good old manual labor. Yep. Feed you a meal or two and put you to work. Can't beat that plan."

"Patty, look," David said. "I shouldn't have spoken to you the way I did. I was so harsh. I don't know what would have happened if you hadn't given Sarah Ann and me a place to stay while I was waiting for my…" He glanced at Tucker. "You know, for things to return to normal so I could tend to my daughter properly. I'm very grateful to you for what you've done for us."

"But you're questioning my motives for doing it," Patty said, not meeting his gaze. She shook her head. "I don't wish to discuss this further. Come on, Tucker, I'll push you on the swing while David scrubs the carpet so you won't be in his way."

"'Kay," Tucker said, then wiggled to get down.

Patty set him on his feet and he took off at a run for the back door, with his mother following slowly behind him. David watched them go, then went down the hallway and settled Sophia in her crib. He checked on Sarah Ann, sitting on the end of the bed and watching her sleep for a while, frowning as he saw the unnatural flush on her cheeks. With a sigh, he returned to the living room to scrub the carpet.

The weekend turned into a blur of misery.

Tucker complained of a tummy ache after lunch and Patty rushed him to the bathroom, but not quite in time. Sarah Ann wasn't able to keep anything down, and by evening Sophia was fussy and refused to eat.

The washing machine and dryer ran constantly with loads of sheets and clothes, and whining little ones clung to any adult willing to hold and rock them. Through the entire day and night the three patients were never asleep at the same time.

Sunday was a rerun, with Patty and David nearly staggering with fatigue. Early Sunday evening, both Tucker and Sarah Ann consumed chicken soup and toast fingers and asked for second helpings. Sophia gobbled a bottle. Temperatures were normal, smiles returned to small faces and Popsicles were awarded to Sarah Ann and Tucker for being so brave while that nasty bug had visited them.

When all three of the children were tucked in for the night and sound asleep, Patty sank onto the end of the sofa, rested her head on the top of it and closed her eyes. David sat down at the opposite end and ran one hand over his beard-roughened face.

"I didn't shave all weekend," he said. "I just realized that. I managed to shower but…well, that was quite a marathon. I guess we all survived. Correct that. The short people are fine. The vote is still out on the tall folks. I'm beat, and I imagine you're exhausted, too."

"Mmm," Patty said, not opening her eyes.

"I think we should pat ourselves on the back for a job well done," David went on. "We beat the bug, and all is right with the world…meaning no one is throwing up all over us. We're a good team, Patty. We got into a routine, hit our stride and the kids' needs were met with no one feeling neglected."

"Mmm." Patty still didn't open her eyes. "There's never been any question regarding our abilities—" she yawned "—as parents, as a mother and father. That arena is not where we fall short, David. It is not where we have major flaws."

"You know what my flaw is," he said tentatively. "Are you going to share yours with me? Don't you think it's time you did?"

"No. What's the point? You don't believe in anything I do or say, so forget it. I'm too tired to get into it. I wouldn't discuss it if I wasn't too tired. We really don't have anything to say to each other, David."

David opened his mouth to deny that that was true,

then snapped it closed in the next instant, shaking his head.

Patty was right, he thought dismally. What could he say to her? That he really didn't doubt her, wasn't wondering what she secretly wanted from him, had thought it over and realized she was exactly who she presented herself to be, a woman of warmth and caring and…

He couldn't say those things because his brain was hammering the doubts at him over and over, questioning his ability to know what was honest and real. But also beating against his mind and his heart was the knowledge that he hated knowing he'd hurt Patty by what he'd said to her. That knowledge twisted his gut into a painful knot when he relived the scene where he'd hurled his accusations at her.

What should he do? Say he was sorry he'd caused her such upset, but that he had to admit he'd meant what he'd said? Sick. Really lame. Patty wouldn't accept an apology from him anyway because she'd know he still doubted the motives for her actions.

The best, the kindest thing he could do was to get out of Patty's way, take his daughter home where they belonged and allow Patty to get on with her life with Tucker and Sophia.

David swept his gaze over the living room.

But he didn't want to leave, he thought. The five of them had functioned like a family here, with so much laughter it filled the place to overflowing. They had been father bear, mother bear and three little baby bears, all of them flourishing, smiling, loving and hugging. There were so many great memories of the time spent here, including lovemaking shared with

Patty so beautiful it defied description. Everything had been perfect.

Until his mind had pushed the amnesia into oblivion and he'd remembered who he was, why he was raising Sarah Ann as a single father, and the fact that he would always be a man alone because of his glaring and hateful flaw.

The sunny, happy bubble within these walls had burst, casting a dark shadow over everything. It was definitely time to go.

"Patty," he said, staring at the far wall. "Tomorrow morning I'm going to pack up our stuff and take Sarah Ann home." He waited for a reply that didn't come, then turned to look at Patty. "Patty?" He narrowed his eyes. "She's sound asleep. Oh, man, she's so worn out and it was my kid who started this audition for a segment of *ER.*"

David wobbled himself to his feet, moved to the end of the sofa and, once he was sure he was steady on the walking cast, slid one arm beneath Patty's knees, the other across her back and lifted her into his arms. She stirred, then settled, her head nestled on his chest, her breathing even as she slept on.

Oh, look at her, David thought. She was so pretty, absolutely lovely, like a fresh, summer day. She felt so good, so right, here in his arms, seemed to weigh hardly more than stocky little Tucker.

She was sleeping so peacefully, just as Sarah Ann, Tucker and Sophia were. The sleep of the innocent.

David frowned, his hold on Patty tightening slightly as he continued to gaze at her face.

How could he have doubted her? he asked himself. How could he entertain, even for a moment, the devastating thought that she had a master plan to snag him and his bank account, making it possible for her to stay home with her kids the way she wanted to? How could he think such a thing about pretty, pretty Patty?

Because he had to.

He had to build that wall around his heart higher and higher to assure that he didn't lose his heart to Patty, only to discover later that he had once again been the victim of himself, of his flaw.

But right now he didn't want to dwell on any of that. He just wanted to hold Patty as she slept, drink in the very sight of her, relive the vivid memories of making love with her as they shared the gift they had given each other so reverently.

Patty shifted slightly and David stood statue-still, hardly breathing, not wanting to wake her and end this special moment. She splayed one hand on his chest and a whispered word escaped from her lips.

"David."

The softly spoken sound of his name suffused David with a warmth like nothing he had ever felt before. It touched his beleaguered mind and quieted the turmoil there, then moved to his heart and encircled it, encasing it in the warmth, filling it with joy and wonder…and love.

Oh, God, no, he thought frantically. This was *not* happening to him. He was *not* in love with Patty Clark. She was not big enough, strong enough, to push past the wall surrounding the essence of his soul. No.

Ah, damn it, yes.

Heaven help him because he loved her, was *in* love

with her with an intensity that seemed to be stealing the very breath from his body. There was nowhere to hide from that truth, from the knowledge that he had failed to protect himself and was a victim of his own inadequacy. He had fallen in love with a woman while not even knowing if she was who she presented herself to be.

The only defense that he had, David thought, sweat beading his brow, was silence. Patty would never know how he felt about her. He would leave here tomorrow, literally run for his life to the house across town where he would live with his daughter. Just the two of them.

The memories of Patty would fade in time, his feelings for her would diminish, then finally no longer exist. He would win this battle with his silence.

David made his way down the hallway with Patty in his arms, and once in her room placed her gently on the bed. He snapped on the lamp on the nightstand, removed her shoes, then covered her with a soft, knitted afghan that lay across the foot of the bed, ignoring the slight trembling of his hands.

He stared at her for a long moment, then narrowed his eyes in self-disgust as he felt an achy sensation close his throat. He turned off the light and crossed the room, hesitating in the doorway for a second, then continuing on without looking back.

Fingers of sunlight tiptoed across Patty's face, insisting that she waken and greet the new day. She opened her eyes slowly to see that the drapes had not been pulled across the window. She glanced at the clock that announced it was 7:22 a.m., then sat bolt upward as she realized she was wearing jeans and a blouse and not her nightshirt. She shook her head slightly, attempting to dispel the last cobwebs of sleep and figure out what was going on.

She had been sitting on the sofa last night, she thought. Tired. Oh, goodness, she had been weary to the bone. David had settled onto the other end of the sofa and they'd had some inane conversation about surviving the crisis of the sick kids and what dynamite parents they were, or some such thing.

And that was it. That was all she remembered— just sitting there like a deflated balloon and wondering vaguely how she was going to get the energy to walk down the hallway and prepare for bed.

Apparently, she mused dryly, she hadn't managed to do that. She must have conked out right there in the living room and David had either led her or carried her to the bed, removed her shoes and that was that.

Wait a minute. David had been just as exhausted as she was but he'd obviously gotten up in the night and fed Sophia. Oh, wasn't that thoughtful? Just so nice of him.

Patty looked at the open doorway of the bedroom.

It certainly was quiet, she thought. Everyone must still be asleep. That was good. It would give her a chance to shower and put on fresh clothes, then prepare waffles for breakfast to celebrate the returned health of the patients and to thank David for his kindness of the previous night. Excellent.

Patty slid off the bed, gathered clean clothes and headed for the bathroom and a warm, welcoming shower. She was smiling when she emerged half an hour later, but the smile vanished instantly as she heard Tucker shrieking in the distance.

"No! No! No!" her son was yelling. "You can't. I won't lets you do that. I'm telling my mommy on you, David. I am, I am."

"Good heavens," Patty said, hurrying from the room. "What's going on?"

She followed the noise to the room shared by Tucker and Sarah Ann, taking in the scene before her in one visual sweep. Sophia was lying on a blanket on Tucker's bed, happily waving her hands in the air. Tucker was in the middle of the room, his little arms crossed firmly across his chest. Sarah Ann stood next to him, her bottom lip trembling.

And an open suitcase was on Sarah Ann's bed, partially filled with clothes as more were added by David.

"What..." Patty said, then stopped speaking because she knew the answer to the question she had been about to ask.

David was leaving, she thought. He was packing Sarah Ann's belongings and preparing to take his daughter home. David was leaving. Tucker was pitching the fit of the century, Sarah Ann was about to burst into tears and...David was leaving. David was leaving.

"Mommy," Tucker said, running to Patty and throwing himself against her legs, causing her to stagger. "David is taking Sarah Ann away, and she's my bestis friend, and I told him I won't lets him do that. Tell him, Mommy. Tell him he can't go."

Of course David couldn't go, couldn't leave, Patty thought rather giddily. What an absurd idea. He belonged here, with them, with—oh, dear God—yes, with her. Where was David's brain this morning, for crying out loud? Didn't he realize they were a family, mother bear and father bear and three little baby bears? Father bears didn't pack suitcases and shuffle off to Buffalo with one of the baby bears.

"Mommy?" Tucker said, sniffling as he looked up at her.

Patty blinked and returned to the moment at hand with a jarring and chilling thud.

"Tucker, honey," she said. "You knew this was going to happen and now it is. It's time for David and Sarah Ann to go to the house where they really live. They were only visiting here."

"No," Tucker said, shoving away from Patty.

"No," Sarah Ann said, and then the tears started. Not to be ignored, Sophia began to wail.

"Ah, hell," David said, throwing up his hands.

"Don't swear in front of the children," Patty said, then paused. "I didn't realize that you had decided on the exact time you planned to…to leave, David."

He hadn't, David thought, until he discovered he'd fallen in love with Patty. He had to get out of there, put distance between them now.

"There's no sense in postponing it," he said, dropping more clothes into Sarah Ann's suitcase. "These kids are going to go nuts whether it happens this morning, or this afternoon, or tomorrow."

"Yes," Patty said quietly. "I suppose you're right. But you don't have a housekeeper to prepare your meals."

"I'll call an agency once we get home and put

things in motion to have them send people over for me to interview.''

''Oh.'' Patty sighed. ''Well, at least have a decent breakfast before you leave.''

''Pardon me?'' David said.

''Hey, you guys,'' Patty said. ''Stop that crying this very minute. David and I can't even hear each other speak. Who wants to help me make waffles?''

''Me,'' Tucker and Sarah Ann said in unison.

''Fine.'' Patty scooped up Sophia from the bed. ''You can pour things in the bowl and take turns stirring. Off we go. Let's march like soldiers. One—two—three—four.''

Patty disappeared with the soldiers stomping behind her in time with the count.

Well, David thought, tossing some socks in the suitcase, Patty certainly wasn't broken up over the departure of the Montgomerys. Let's march like soldiers and blah, blah, blah. It was no big deal to her if he left with Sarah Ann except for the fact that she'd be stuck with a pouting Tucker.

Wouldn't Patty miss them—him? Wouldn't she think about how nice it had been to interact like a family during all these days they'd been together? And what about the nights? The sharing of the gift, the beautiful lovemaking? Huh? What about that, Patty Clark?

David sank onto the edge of Tucker's bed and stared into space.

His mind was running in circles again, he thought dismally. He was getting bent out of shape because Patty didn't seem to give a rip that he and Sarah Ann were leaving. But if she burst into tears, begged him not to go, told him how important he had become to her, the whole nine yards, he would immediately doubt her sincerity, wonder if her performance was as phony as a three-dollar bill.

Oh, yeah, no doubt about it. He had to get out of here. He was in love with the Patty he wanted her to be, but he didn't know if that was really who Patty was.

"I'm hitting the road," David said, getting to his feet. "Now."

Breakfast was a dismal affair with Tucker and Sarah Ann whining as they glared at David. Tucker spilled his milk on top of his waffle. Sarah Ann refused to eat even one bite of her food. Patty and David's waffles got cold and hard as they attempted to cheer up the sniffling three-year-olds. Sophia, at least, finished her bottle and fell asleep as though announcing she'd had enough of this nonsense.

David chalked up the meal as a lost cause and left the table to finish packing his and Sarah Ann's clothes. He took the suitcases to his vehicle, then lifted a crying Sarah Ann into his arms.

"Say thank you and goodbye, Sarah Ann," he said, raising his voice to be heard over her wailing.

"No," she yelled. "I don't wants to go. No."

"No, no, no," Tucker said, stamping one foot.

"Tucker, stop it," Patty said.

"Patty, I am so grateful for…" David started, then stopped as his daughter stiffened in his arms and he had to struggle to maintain his hold on her.

"I understand," Patty said, nodding. "You're welcome. I just wish… That is… Goodbye, David."

David looked directly into her eyes for a long moment before he spoke.

"Goodbye, Patty," he said finally, then turned and left the house, Sarah Ann wailing all the way.

Tucker flopped onto the floor and kicked his feet, screaming at the top of his lungs. Patty spun around and went into the kitchen to clean up the mess on the table, totally ignoring her son's dramatic performance.

Go for it, Tucker, she thought, carrying two plates to the counter. He was expressing exactly how he felt about Sarah Ann and David leaving and more power to him.

And you, Patty Sharpe Clark? she asked herself, returning to the table for more plates. She'd just said a breezy "Goodbye, David" as though he was going to the store for milk and would be back in half an hour. So long, David. Ta-ta. Farewell. Adios.

Patty sniffled.

Yes, David was gone, she thought. Gone, gone, gone. But the terrifying fact she was facing right there in her kitchen as she juggled sticky, syrupy plates of gross-looking waffles was that when David had walked out of her home he had taken her heart with him.

At least he didn't know the truth, the depth of her feelings, but she did. Oh, yes, she did. And she wanted to crawl into bed, pull the blankets over her head and cry for a week.

Because she had fallen in love with David Montgomery.

Chapter Twelve

By early afternoon Patty felt as though the walls of the house were closing in on her, making her edgy and irritable.

It was just so quiet, she thought, despite the fact that there were two children in the house. To suddenly reduce the numbers in a family—no, not a family—a group of people from five to three required some adjusting, especially when one of said missing was a busy three-year-old.

And especially when the other no-longer-there-person was the man she loved and wished to heaven that she didn't.

Tucker was not helping the level of tension one iota as he continued to whine and complain about his bestis friend Sarah Ann being gone, and it wasn't fair, and he was mad at everybody, just everybody in the whole wide world.

Patty finally loaded the kids into the car and took them to the park. When they returned home, Tucker was more than ready for his nap and Patty made a big production out of allowing him to snuggle into her bed, her actual motive being that she needed to clean the room Tucker had shared with Sarah Ann, which was a mess after David's packing spree. With both children asleep, Patty blanked her mind of any gloomy thoughts and tackled the project.

When she pulled the sheets from Sarah Ann's bed so they could be washed, Patches the bear tumbled to the floor.

"Oh, great," Patty said aloud, snatching up the shabby toy.

She plunked down on the edge of Tucker's bed and stared at the bear that still boasted a bandage of duct tape.

Sarah Ann was already upset about leaving here, she thought. When bedtime came and it was discovered that Patches was not there, the little miss would no doubt bring down the roof.

Oh, what to do, what to do? She could, she supposed, protect her own fragile emotions and mail the bear to Sarah Ann tomorrow. No, that would be rotten. The image in her mind of that sweet child crying herself to sleep because Patches had been left behind was grim, very bad. Patty sighed, then narrowed her eyes and told herself to get a plan.

"Got it," she said, a few moments later.

She was not prepared to see David so soon after discovering that she was in love with him. Oh, no. No way. Must not happen. So. She'd put Patches in a plastic bag from the grocery store, sneak up to the

Montgomery front door and tie the bag on the knob. Upon returning home she'd have Tucker telephone Sarah Ann and tell her where precious Patches was.

And why could Tucker not get out of the car and visit his bestis friend? His crummy mother would lie through her teeth and tell him that Sarah Ann was napping and polite people did not disturb those who were sleeping.

"Not bad," Patty said, nodding decisively. "My nose will grow, but that's the way it goes."

When Tucker appeared after his snooze, Patty explained that she had found Patches in the bedclothes. Yes, they must return Sarah Ann's favorite toy to her immediately, but, my, my, look at the time. Sarah Ann was napping. The grocery bag was produced, the plan laid out, and before Tucker could complain, Sophia was retrieved from her crib and they were off on their mission.

The closer they came to David's house, the bigger the knot in Patty's stomach grew. She was so furious with herself for having lost her heart to David, and she needed time, time, time to deal with the hopelessness of it all, to begin somehow to push the memories of him from her mind and heart. She certainly wasn't prepared to see him just hours after he had left her home, that was for sure.

At David's house, Patty turned off the ignition, then whispered to Tucker that she would be right back. She snatched up the plastic bag and ran to the front door. Bending over as though that would make her closer to invisible, Patty leaned forward and began to tie the bag onto the knob. She had nearly completed the task when the front door swung open.

Patty was so startled she toppled over, landing on all fours in front of David. She cringed, then looked up and up and farther up to see his frowning face.

"Well, hi," she said, forcing a smile to materialize.

"What are you doing?" David said. "Are you suddenly into peeping through keyholes?"

"Don't be silly," Patty said, getting to her feet with less than graceful form. "Patches got left behind and I was returning it without disturbing Sarah Ann's nap by ringing the doorbell."

"Sarah Ann isn't napping."

"She could have been," Patty said, planting her hands on her hips.

"Is that your story and you're sticking to it?" David said. "Or could it be that you're attempting to avoid seeing me?"

"Why would I do that?" Patty said, concentrating on straightening her T-shirt over the waistband of her jeans. "Gotta go. Kids in the car."

"Tucker," Sarah Ann yelled, appearing in the doorway. She zoomed out the door and headed for the car. "Tucker, Tucker, you came to visit."

"No, Sarah Ann," Patty called after her. "We didn't come to visit. We just wanted to bring Patches to you so that... Darn it."

"If you drive off now I'll have to go through another tantrum thing with Sarah Ann," David said wearily. "You'd better come in for a few minutes."

"Gosh," Patty said dryly, "how could I refuse such a gracious invitation."

David sighed. "I'm sorry. That sounded rude. The truth of the matter is, Patty, that it's going to take some time to adjust to being here. You know, just me and Sarah Ann. We…she…okay…*we* will miss you. And Tucker and Sophia.''

''We'll miss you, too, David,'' she said, meeting his gaze. ''Very much. You…you and Sarah Ann.''

They continued to look into each other's eyes, each ticking second bringing a memory of precious sharing to the fronts of their minds. And with the memories came the desire and the heat. And the secrets kept of their love for each other that couldn't, wouldn't, be spoken in words.

Patty finally tore her gaze from David's, ignoring her racing heart and the heat pulsing low in her body.

''Would you like a glass of lemonade?'' David said, his voice gritty. ''A quick snack might satisfy the kids as far as being an official visit.''

''Yes, all right,'' Patty said. ''I'll go get Tucker and Sophia out of the car. I have the baby locks in place and Tucker can't open the back door.''

A short time later the group was at the large kitchen table with glasses of lemonade and a plate of rather stale store-bought cookies. Sophia was on the table in her carrier.

''I have three interviews set up for housekeepers tomorrow,'' David said. ''I'll keep Sarah Ann home from the Fuzzy Bunny because I want to see how these women interact with her.''

Patty nodded.

''Before I forget,'' he went on, ''I want to thank you for making the effort to bring Patches over here. Bedtime would have been a disaster without that bear.''

Patty nodded.

"Let's go to my room, Tucker," Sarah Ann said, sliding off of her chair.

"'Kay," Tucker said.

"Ten minutes. That's it," David said. "And there will be no fussing when it's time for Tucker to go home. Right, Patty?"

Patty nodded.

The pair ran from the room and Patty stared at Sophia's foot that was waving in the air as though it was the most fascinating foot Patty had ever seen.

"Is there some reason why you aren't speaking?" David said.

Because she was a breath away from crying, that's why, Patty thought frantically. She could feel the achy sensation in her throat and the tears stinging the back of her eyes. She was sitting across the table from the man she'd fallen in love with, and he'd never know how she felt. She had nothing to offer him, nothing.

Oh, sure, she could be a terrific mother to his daughter but so would the woman he hired as a house-keeper. He'd pay someone to be there to hug and hold Sarah Ann. But the role of wife was far, far different.

She was also assuming that David had deep feelings for her and would even *want* her to be his wife, which was probably ridiculous. Oh, yes, she was about to cry and she wanted to go home.

Patty sniffled. "My allergies are acting up. That's why I'm not saying much. Talking aggravates my allergies. Unusual, but true. Yep, my allergies are very strange."

"You never mentioned that you're bothered by allergies."

"Didn't I? Well, I am. Sometimes. I just never

know when they're going to give me fits.'' Patty got
to her feet. "Well, we must go. Thank you for the
snack. Good luck tomorrow with the interviews. I'm
sure you'll find someone who is perfect for the job.
Someone who loves children, who will realize there's
more to do here than cook and clean. Someone who
will meet Sarah Ann's emotional needs as well as the
basic physical ones.''

"The way you did," David said, looking directly
at her.

"That was different, David. You're now talking
about paying someone to do what I did from my
heart. Sarah Ann will know if the woman is sincere.
It's so important that…I'm sorry. I'm lecturing you
and it's none of my business. It's just that I love your
daughter…'' *And you.* "…and I want her…" *And
you.* "…to be happy."

And I love you, Patty Clark, David thought as he
rose and came around the table. She wasn't having
an allergy attack. That trembling in her voice, the
shimmering in her eyes, was caused by tears. She was
crying and he didn't know why and he hated to see
her upset and… Oh, hell.

David closed the distance between them, gripped
Patty's shoulders, lowered his head and kissed her so
intensely that Patty was convinced she was going to
faint dead away. Then the kiss gentled and she leaned
into it, savoring it and every wondrous sensation
sweeping through her body.

Oh, David, David, David, her mind hummed.

Patty, David's mind thundered.

He broke the kiss and released her, slowly and so
very reluctantly.

"I shouldn't have done that," he said, hearing the raspy quality to his voice. "I'm sorry."

"I'm not," Patty said dreamily, then blinked. "I mean, I…I accept your apology and… Oh, forget it." She went to the side of the table and lifted Sophia's carrier. "Would you call the kids downstairs, please? We really must go. Oh, and don't forget to retrieve Patches from the doorknob.

"Patty…"

"I can't talk anymore. Allergies."

Patty hurried from the room and went to the front door where she counted down the seconds until she could escape from this house, knowing she still didn't have a clue how to retrieve her heart from David Montgomery.

The exit was a blur and Tucker pouted all the way home because he wanted to play longer with his bestis friend. Patty just sniffled and decided she just didn't have the energy to attempt to do her cheerleader-mother routine to bring a smile to her son's face.

The remainder of the day dragged by, and with a grateful sigh Patty finally read a story to Tucker and kissed him good-night. She fed Sophia, then shortly afterward went to bed herself where she was finally able to give way to the tears that had been threatening for hours.

She cried until she was exhausted, then finally slept, only to wake at dawn and realize that she'd dreamed of David.

The next day David hired the second woman he interviewed for the job of housekeeper. Rosa was a plump Italian woman in her mid-forties with sparkling dark eyes and a hearty laugh. She was widowed, and her children and grandchildren were scattered across the country.

When she invited Sarah Ann to sit on her lap, the little girl hesitated only a moment, then extended her arms to Rosa to be lifted up and snuggled. Sarah Ann proceeded to tell Rosa that Tucker was Sarah Ann's bestis friend, she missed him, and she missed Patty and Sophia, and so did her daddy because his eyes didn't smile anymore.

"Oh?" Rosa said, then looked at David questioningly.

"Long story," David said, then cleared his throat. "Let's settle on the hours you'll work. Okay?"

It was agreed that Rosa would arrive after lunch, tend to the house and laundry, then pick Sarah Ann up at the Fuzzy Bunny about four o'clock. Rosa would prepare dinner, serve it, then clean the kitchen before going home.

"I'll be out looking for office space, then setting up my new law practice once I find what I want," David said. "Down the road, when I have some clients, I might have to work late occasionally but I don't intend to make a habit of it. Sarah Ann comes first with me."

"And this Tucker, Patty and Sophia?" Rosa said. "Will they be visiting? Having dinner with you sometimes? I don't mind cooking extra because it reminds me of when I had my family around me."

"I... Um..." David said.

"Daddy?" Sarah Ann said, sliding off Rosa's lap and staring at her father. "Aren't they going to come to visit and eat dinner and do stuff and everything? I miss them and I know you do, too. I know, I know, I know. You like them lots 'cause you hug them and kiss them and stuff. You give Patty mommy-kisses. Those are different from kid-kisses.''

''What?'' David said, his eyes widening.

''We sawed you. Me and Tucker. You and Patty were doing a mommy-and-daddy kiss in the kitchen.''

Rosa laughed in delight as David felt a warm flush creep up his neck.

''Not to worry,'' Rosa said. ''There's always extra food on Rosa's stove for company.''

''Good,'' Sarah Ann said decisively. ''Then Tucker and Patty and Sophia can come lots of times to eat with us.''

''I'm not taking part in this discussion,'' David said, rolling his eyes heavenward.

It was agreed that Rosa would start work at the Montgomery home the following Monday, giving David the remainder of the week to finish unpacking the boxes still scattered through the house.

By Thursday afternoon David admitted defeat. Sarah Ann had whined and fussed since Rosa had left the house on Tuesday. She had nothing to do and no one to play with, Sarah Ann moaned dramatically. Why couldn't Tucker come over and play? Why couldn't Daddy quit doing stuff with those boxes and push her on the swings? Why couldn't she go to Tucker's house for a play date?

David called the Fuzzy Bunny and informed them that Sarah Ann Montgomery would be attending the day-care center on a daily basis again, beginning tomorrow. He anticipated, however, he told the woman he spoke to, that Sarah Ann might have a rocky readjustment due to the fact that her "bestis" friend Tucker Clark would not be there to play with her.

"We're accustomed to handling situations like that, Mr. Montgomery," the woman said. "Don't worry about a thing. We'll see you and Sarah Ann in the morning."

In the middle of the next morning, David carried a kicking and screaming Sarah Ann into the Fuzzy Bunny and set her on her feet. She immediately dissolved into a heap on the floor and wailed.

"Sarah Ann," David said. "Stop it right this minute."

"I wants Tucker," she yelled. "Tucker, Tucker, Tucker."

Susan hurried to greet the pair.

"Hi, Sarah Ann," she said cheerfully. "How's things down there on the floor?" She looked at David. "She'll be fine. She'll connect with another child and won't miss Tucker so much once she gets involved in play." She paused. "So, how's Patty?"

"Patty?" David said.

"Patty Clark?" Susan said. "Who rushed to your rescue and played Florence Nightingale because you had amnesia? Took you home and nursed you back to memory and health? That Patty? My cousin is a nurse at the hospital."

"Oh," David said, nodding. "I see. Well, um, Patty and her children are fine, and I'm very, very grateful for all that she did for me and Sarah Ann, believe me. My memory returned, I have this manageable walking cast, and Sarah Ann and I are back in our own home."

Susan sighed. "And Patty's raising those two little ones alone. I'd like to give that ex-husband of hers a piece of my mind. The thing that really disturbs me, though, is that Patty is determined never to marry again. She plans to devote herself to her children and that is that. I've argued the point with her until I'm blue in the face and she won't budge."

"What?" David said, leaning forward slightly.

Susan moved closer to him to be heard over Sarah Ann, who was setting time records for hollering.

"It's true," Susan said. "She's going to be both mother and father to those kids and won't even entertain the idea that a wonderful man might come into her life and wish to marry her. She doesn't want any part of that scene again. No way. It's such a shame. She's only thirty years old and has so much to offer a man and... Enough of this. Sarah Ann isn't going to stop this racket until you leave. See you later, Mr. Montgomery."

"Yes. Fine," David said, frowning as his mind echoed with the words that Susan had just spoken. He looked at Sarah Ann. "Are you sure you want me to leave when she's acting like that?"

"Oh, yes. Go." Susan flapped her hands at him. "She'll stop before you get out of the parking lot."

David nodded and left the building, later only vaguely able to remember the drive home. In his kitchen he sat down at the table with a glass of orange juice and mentally replayed yet again what Susan had said.

Patty is determined never to marry again...doesn't want any part of that scene...she's going to be both mother and father to those kids.

Was it feasible, David thought, his mind racing, that his doubts about Patty were unfounded? He'd automatically questioned her motives for being so kind to him and to his daughter, wondering if her real agenda was to snag a money-machine-man who would make it possible for her to stay home to raise her children as she had always planned to do.

Had he transferred the lingering pain of Marsha's betrayal and deceit onto Patty and declared her to be a carbon copy of his wife simply because she was a woman? He'd convinced himself that he had a major flaw, couldn't determine whether a woman, any woman ever, was who she presented herself to be.

Maybe...maybe?...that wasn't true? He had made one horrific mistake in believing in Marsha, but that didn't necessarily mean that every member of the female species was cut from the same cloth, for heaven's sake. Perhaps he'd been too hard on himself and had, therefore, slam-dunked Patty due to his own lack of confidence.

She didn't want his money or his muscles, David thought, feeling the color drain from his face, or his extra set of hands to help carry the load of raising children. Patty didn't want anything from him at all but the short-term sharing of the gift they had agreed upon. He was now probably out of sight, out of mind as far as Patty Clark was concerned. And to reinforce that attitude of hers, big-mouth him had put her under a bare lightbulb and demanded to know what she was truly after.

"Ohhh, no," David said with a groan, as he dragged both hands down his face. "What have I done? I love that woman. I'm in love with Patty, damn it.''

Patty is determined never to marry again.

''We'll see about *that*,'' David said, getting to his feet.

He had to talk to Patty. He had to tell her how very sorry he was for judging her so harshly and beg her to forgive him. He had to lay his heart and pride on the line and ask her if she was in love with him just as he was with her.

And if she did love him, he was going to ask her to marry him, be his wife, his partner in life.

David strode toward the front door, sweeping his gaze over the house as he went.

This would be a home, a real home, he thought. Laughter would ring through these rooms. Sarah Ann and Tucker would scatter their toys everywhere as they played together as bestis friends and brother and sister. Sophia would speak her first words here, take her first steps.

And down the road if it was meant to be, there would be another child, one created by the gift, the love shared in the private darkness of night between Mr. and Mrs. Montgomery. David and Patty. Oh, yeah, that was a warm and wonderful image being painted in his mind.

As David drove toward Patty's he realized that he was becoming more tense with every passing mile. His future happiness was going to be determined by what transpired during this meeting with Patty. The rest of his life was hanging in the balance here.

Oh, great, he thought, as he stopped at a red light. He was now a wreck, was coming unglued, big-time.

If he blew this, if he couldn't find the proper words to… Get a grip, Montgomery. He was an attorney who was trained to maintain his cool and articulate his case with expertise.

He would sit Patty down, start at the top and speak from his heart. She would listen, really hear what he was saying, declare her love for him and agree to become his wife. Yes. That's how it would go…if he didn't have a nervous breakdown before he could get to Patty's house.

A horn blared behind David's vehicle and he jerked, then pressed on the gas as he saw that the light was now green and he was still sitting there like a dolt.

I'm calm, I'm calm, I'm calm, he mentally chanted in his mind during the miles remaining from here to the rest of his life.

David slowed as he turned onto Patty's street and slowed even more as he approached her house. He frowned as he saw a vehicle in her driveway and made the instant decision to park in front of the neighboring house to wait until whoever was visiting her left.

The minutes ticked slowly by. His tension built with every thud of his heart. He clenched his jaw and tapped his fingers impatiently on the steering wheel, his gaze riveted on Patty's front door. Then at last, the door opened and David stiffened, every muscle in his body tightening.

Patty came out of the house onto the small porch with tall, good-looking man who appeared to be part Asian. They were smiling, and in the next instant, they were hugging each other in a long, obviously heartfelt embrace.

"What... Oh, God, no," David said, his voice a harsh whisper.

The old but not forgotten pain of betrayal slammed against him like a physical blow, making it difficult to breathe. The agony was followed in a rush by wrath, rip-roaring fury at himself for believing that his being taken in by Marsha was a one-time mistake. And anger burned deep within him toward Patty because his doubts, his questions about her were justified.

"Damn it," David said, ignoring the achy sensation in his throat.

Before he even realized that he was moving, he left his vehicle and with long, heavy strides started toward the couple on the porch.

Chapter Thirteen

As David continued his determined, albeit somewhat clumsy approach to Patty's house due to his cast, the couple moved off the porch and started toward the vehicle in the driveway. Patty had her arm slipped through the man's and she was smiling up at him. David narrowed his eyes and trudged on. Patty finally saw him as he neared the rear of the vehicle.

"David," she said, surprise evident on her face and in her voice. She dropped her arm to her side. "What are you doing here?"

"My arrival is a tad inconvenient, isn't it?" David said, a pulse beating in his temple. "And to think that I sat in my kitchen drinking orange juice and came to the conclusion that I was wrong about you, had made you pay the price for a mistake—one mistake—I made in my past. Oh, no, I told myself, I now realize that Patty is real and honest and everything that I believe her to be.''

"I—'' Patty said.

"I'm speaking here,'' David snapped, causing Patty and the man to jerk at his outburst. "Patty doesn't have an agenda, a crummy motive of wanting my money and my willingness to help with the kids so she can stay home like she wants to and be a full-time mother. Not my Patty. Hell, no.

"Well, here I am, and isn't this just a pop in the chops, a reality check big-time? Why am I here? Oh, what a joke. I came to apologize, beg your forgiveness for ever doubting you. I came to tell you that I love you, damn it, and I want to marry you.

"What?'' Patty said, her eyes widening.

"But I should never have had that conversation with myself while I was drinking orange juice because now I know the ugly truth. You were stringing me along the whole time, and not only that, you were involved with another man while you were doing it.''

He pointed at the man next to Patty. "Don't try to deny any of this, Patty Clark, because there he is in living, breathing color. I saw the hug and the smiles and the... God, I am such a fool. Well, so what if I'm in love with you. It's no big deal. I'll get over it. No problem. None. I'm outta here. Goodbye.''

"Excuse me,'' the man next to Patty said pleasantly. "Might I have a word?''

"There's nothing you can say that I'm interested in hearing,'' David said, none too quietly.

"Well, all I wanted to do was introduce myself,'' the man said. "I'm...'' He stifled a laugh. "I'm Ryan

Sharpe. Patty's brother. Listen closely, please. That's *brother*, not *lover*. Brother.''

David opened his mouth to reply, snapped it closed again, then planted his hands on his hips and stared at the heavens.

''Beam me up, Scotty,'' he said. ''Forget it. Nobody wants to associate with an idiot.'' He shook his head. ''I don't believe what I just did.''

''It was well done, I must say,'' Ryan said, giving way to his laughter. ''I thought I was going to end up with a broken nose. Now, then, I'm not needed in this fascinating discussion so I'll shove off and allow you two to straighten out your differences.

''I'm assuming you're *the* David Montgomery I've been hearing so much about since I got back into town. It was…interesting meeting you, David.'' Ryan kissed Patty on the forehead. ''Talk to you later, sis. Love ya.''

''I love you, too, Ryan,'' Patty said. ''Thanks for coming by.''

As Ryan backed his vehicle out of the driveway, David made a quick list of ten places he'd rather be than standing there in front of Patty Sharpe Clark— Patty, who was now folding her arms tightly beneath her breasts and glowering at him with such obvious anger he was back to begging Scotty to beam him up.

''Well,'' David said, then cleared his throat. ''When I blow it I really do a helluva job, don't I? Yep.'' He paused and sighed. ''Patty, I am so sorry for what I just did and said.''

''Come into the house,'' she said, spinning around. ''We've given the neighbors enough of a show for one day. And keep your voice down inside because the kids are napping.''

''He doesn't look like he's your brother,'' David muttered, as he followed Patty.

''Ryan is adopted, you dope,'' Patty said, entering the living room. ''He's half Korean, and he's the best brother anyone could ever hope to have.'' She sank onto a chair.

''Oh. May I sit down?''

''Whatever.''

David sank onto the sofa and dragged his hands down his face.

''Could I start over,'' he said, ''with what I wanted to say to you, go all the way back to the light that dawned while I was drinking my orange juice?''

''Whatever.''

''Ah, Patty, I know I really messed things up outside, but I'm still on shaky ground emotionally with all that I've discovered about myself. That's really no excuse for what I did out there but I meant what I said. I love you with all my heart, my soul, with all that I am. I was making you pay the price for what Marsha did and that was so wrong of me. I realize that now and am begging you to forgive me. You are you. Exactly who you present yourself to be.

''You're a warm and loving, caring and sharing woman and mother, and I want to spend the rest of my life with you. I want to marry you, turn my house into a home, create a baby with you and… Please? Say you forgive me. Say you love me as much as I love you. Do you, Patty? Do you love me?''

Patty looked directly at David, then had to blink away tears that misted her eyes.

"Yes," she whispered. "Yes, David, I love you very, very much."

David closed his eyes for a moment and drew a shuddering breath.

"Thank you," he said, emotion ringing in his voice. He opened his eyes again. "I'm not certain that I deserve you, but I'm not going to argue *that* point. All I know is that I've put the past to rest at long last, and I want to live in the present and future with you as my wife. Will you? Will you be my wife? Will you marry me, Patty Sharpe Clark? Please?"

Patty got to her feet and crossed the room to sit next to David on the sofa. She smiled at him, tears shimmering in her eyes.

"Will you make love with me, David? Now? Before the kids wake up from their naps? Will you share our beautiful gift with me again?" Patty leaned forward and brushed her lips over David's, causing a bolt of heat to course through him. "Please, David, make love with me."

David fully intended to point out the fact that Patty had not given him an answer regarding his proposal of marriage, but when she outlined his lips with a feathery touch from one delicate fingertip, all rational thought fled.

Patty got to her feet, and just as David had done the very first time they had made love, she extended one hand toward him palm up. And in a repeat motion of that long-ago day, David lifted one hand and placed it in Patty's, rising to stand close to her in the next instant.

They went down the hallway, glancing in at a sleeping Tucker and Sophia as they went, then closed the door to Patty's bedroom and the world beyond it behind them.

An urgency engulfed them, the need, the want consuming them, building to a fever pitch with swirling heat and racing hearts. They shed their clothes, David tossed back the blankets on the bed, then they reached for the other and tumbled onto the bed.

"I love you," David said, as he splayed one hand on Patty's stomach.

"I love you, too, David," she whispered.

And with those words the gift they shared took on greater meaning; their emotions were much deeper and more heartfelt than before as they intertwined with the physical ecstasy of their lovemaking. They kissed and caressed, hands never still, lips following where those hands had created a heated path.

Patty's senses heightened and she savored every sensation, feeling womanly and beautiful and so very special. She sighed with pure feminine pleasure as David paid homage to her breasts, laving first one nipple, then the other into taut buttons. She sank her fingers into his thick hair and urged his mouth more firmly onto the soft flesh, closing her eyes to memorize the sensuous moment.

David raised his head to capture Patty's mouth, his muscles bunching, trembling, as want and need pushed him to the edge of his control.

Patty loved him, his mind sang. They were going to have it all. They would be husband and wife, raising their super kids, living in a home, a real home filled with sunshine and laughter and love neverending. Patty loved him. And, oh, how he loved her. There was nothing temporary now about the gift they were sharing. No. It was theirs until death parted them. Because Patty loved him.

He left her only long enough to protect her, then returned to her embrace, kissing her yet again, then meshing their bodies. The rhythm began, so perfectly synchronized it was impossible to tell where one body ended and the other began. They were one. One entity. Soaring to the place, *their* place, that awaited them with the glorious colors and the exquisite release that rippled through each of them seconds apart.

They held fast to each other, not wishing to return from where they had gone, then whispering endearments as they floated slowly and gently back to the bed, the room, the realization that sleeping children could waken at any moment.

"So lovely," Patty said wistfully. "Mmm."

"Yes, it was," David said, his voice still gritty. "I suppose, though, that we'd better get it together here before Tucker comes knocking on the door."

"Mmm," Patty said, her lashes drifting down.

"Hey, no sleeping now, my lady."

Patty laughed. "But I can't move, sir, because my bones have dissolved."

David chuckled, kissed her quickly, then left the bed to gather his clothes.

"I'll take a quick shower," he said, "then head Tucker off at the pass if he gets up while you hit the suds. Okay?"

"Mmm," Patty said, then smiled and sat up. "Okay."

But Tucker was still sleeping soundly when Patty arrived in the living room to find David sitting on the sofa. He patted the cushion next to him and Patty joined him eagerly.

"We need to back up a bit," David said, then kissed the top of Patty's head. "You didn't really answer me when I asked you to marry me. I could get down on one knee if you like, but with this cast I'd be a rather clumsy Prince Charming, I'm afraid. So, I'll just say it again. Patty Clark, will you marry me?"

Patty shifted on the sofa so she could look directly into David's eyes, then drew a shaky breath.

"No, David," she said, a faint echo of tears in her voice. "No, I won't marry you. I can't."

A chill swept through David and he swallowed heavily.

"Why not?" he said. "You love me. I love you. We're crazy about each other's kids. Everything is in place, Patty. We'll live in my house because it's big enough for all of us, and you can stay home the way you want to and raise the munchkins and...I...I don't understand."

"It's because I love you so much, David, that I know I have to refuse your proposal."

"You're not making any sense."

"Oh, yes, I am, I truly am," she said. "You've said that I've been keeping a secret from you and that's true. It's time you knew the truth about me. David, my secret, my horrendous flaw, is not a one-time mistake in judgment as yours was with Marsha. No. Mine is forever, is who I am, or more accurately, who I am not. My flaw would destroy what we have together if we marry."

"I..."

"Please, hear me out," Patty said. "David, I...I am not capable of being a proper wife. I just don't know how, despite how hard I try. I would make you so unhappy, so very miserable, because I'm a failure in that role.

"Yes, I'm a great mother. And our lovemaking has shown me that I'm a woman capable of giving herself to the man she loves with total abandon, as it should be. But as a wife? I am totally inadequate. I drove Peter into the arms of another woman because I didn't know how to meet his needs, be his other half, his partner. What he did wasn't his fault, it was mine. Mine, David."

David shook his head, a deep frown on his face.

"It's true," Patty said, leaning toward him. "I've accepted that truth and I've vowed to never marry again, never destroy another person's dreams.

"I love you, David. I want to be with you whenever it's possible. We'll be lovers as well as the mother bear and the father bear to our baby bears. But you'll live at your house with Sarah Ann and I'll stay here with Tucker and Sophia. I will be everything I can be for you, but I will not be your wife because I love you far, far too much to agree to that."

David took Patty's hands in his.

"There is no way on earth," he said, "that I will ever believe what you're saying. I lived here, remember? You took care of me when I was injured, cheered me up when I was bummed out because I was so frustrated dealing with the amnesia, did everything that a wife would do if her husband was hurt."

"And how many times did you holler at me for

treating you like a child? That wasn't a wife tending to your needs, David, it was a mother.''

"Well—"

"Granted, you showed me, taught me, that I *could* separate the woman from the mother but it stops right there. I am offering myself to you as a woman and as a mother to Sarah Ann. That's all I have to give you. I'm not capable of being a wife.''

"What are you suggesting?" David said. "That we have an affair that lasts twenty or thirty years? Patty, that's nuts.''

"No, it's the way it is.'' Patty's eyes filled with tears. "I know you want a wife, a real family living in your lovely home. I'll understand if you don't want to see me again so you can move past your feelings for me and find someone who can meet your needs. I'm so sorry, David. I wish things were different. I wish *I* was different. But I can't change the facts, the truth.''

This was crazy, David thought frantically. Patty actually believed that it was her fault that her marriage had failed, that Peter the jerk had left her for another woman. No way. He'd wondered if she was harboring that ridiculous conclusion, then dismissed the idea as being out in left field. But now she was telling him that was exactly how she felt. That was her secret, the big flaw? No way.

But he had to be very careful about how he handled this. Patty was very, very fragile on this subject, completely vulnerable. If he hollered his head off and demanded she drop her foolish notion, she was liable to send him packing and tell him not to come back.

Slow and easy, Montgomery.

"Look," he said, "let's table this for now. This is a momentous day because we declared our love for each other. We should savor that, don't you think? We should celebrate. Why don't we go out to dinner tomorrow night? Just the two of us. Do you think you can get a sitter for a Saturday night on such short notice? I don't even know any sitters yet so I guess I'd bring Sarah Ann here and pay your sitter extra to add another kiddo to the heap."

Patty frowned. "You still want to see me, be with me?"

"I love you. I don't turn that emotion off like a faucet just because I didn't get my own way."

"Then you're accepting my terms?" Patty said, swiping an errant tear from her cheek.

"I didn't say that. I said we're tabling the subject for now."

Patty sighed. "I don't know if this is wise. It might be like a dark cloud hanging over us. You'd be hoping that I'll change my mind and I'd be certain that I wouldn't. What's going to make that cloud go away? Nothing."

"We're not dealing with that now. We're going to a fancy restaurant and we'll make a toast to each other, our love for each other, with very expensive wine. That's it."

"Well…"

"Why don't you get on the phone and see if you can find a babysitter?"

"Okay," Patty said, smiling. "It's been so long, months and months, since I got all dressed up and went out to dinner. What time should I say? About seven?"

"Works for me."

Patty went into the kitchen to consult the list of sitters posted on the refrigerator and to use the telephone.

Man, oh, man, David thought, as Patty disappeared from view, what a complicated mess. He should be on top of the world because the woman he loved returned that love in kind. But that rosy bubble had been burst before he'd really had a chance to enjoy his arrival on cloud nine.

Peter Clark had walked out on Patty, left her for another woman, didn't even bother to use his visitation rights to see his own children. But that wasn't his fault? Patty had driven him to desert her because she was such a lousy wife? It was all her fault?

He wasn't buying that. Not in this lifetime. He was gearing up, getting ready to go to battle. He would make Patty see, believe, know, that she would be everything he'd ever hoped to find in a wife. He would win this war and Patty Clark would become Patty Montgomery, wife of David, mother to Sophia, Tucker and Sarah Ann. And a couple more little Montgomerys.

Yep, he would be the victor.

David dragged both hands down his face.

He had to be, he thought. He just had to be because if he wasn't, then the future would spread before him in a dark and stark landscape of loneliness.

Patty returned to the living room to announce that Mrs. Williams, a widow who had sat for the children before, was available tomorrow night and the addition of Sarah Ann was fine with her. Patty and David agreed that he would pick up the woman on his way there.

"I'd better go," David said, getting to his feet. "I've already dealt with one tantrum-throwing kid today who was not happy because Tucker wasn't with her. I think I'll pass on Tucker repeating the performance because I'm here without Sarah Ann."

Patty laughed. "You're a wise man, David Montgomery."

"I know," he said, as he opened the front door. "I fell in love with you, didn't I? Smartest thing I've ever done. I'll see you tomorrow night." He paused. "By the way, do you think your brother is going to inform the entire MacAllister clan about me believing he was your lover instead of your brother?"

"No doubt about it," Patty said, smiling. "Ryan won't be able to resist sharing such a great story."

"I was afraid of that," David said, then dropped a quick kiss on Patty's lips. "Goodbye. I love you. Goodbye. I'll be looking forward to our date. Goodbye."

"Goodbye, David," she said with a burst of laughter.

Patty closed the door behind him, then leaned her back against it, wrapping her hands around her elbows.

The man she loved, she mused, loved her. Unbelievable. And she had just made exquisitely beautiful love with the man she loved who loved her. Fantastic.

But how long would the man she loved settle for less than what he wanted from her?

How long would it be before David walked out of this house for the last time, leaving behind the echo of his goodbye?

Chapter Fourteen

Patty glanced around the lushly furnished restaurant, unable to hide her smile.

"Oh, David," she said, switching her gaze to meet his. "This is like something out of a fairy tale."

"If that's the case," he said, matching her smile, "then you're the princess. I have to say it again. You look beautiful tonight."

"Thank you. You're rather dashing in that suit yourself. We've never seen each other in our all-grown-up clothes before."

And the dress she was wearing, Patty thought, was about four or five years old. But since she'd hardly worn it in the past it didn't look faded and it was, thank goodness, one of those outfits that never went out of style. A pale blue camisole top, blousing over a chiffon skirt that fell just below her knees and swirled around her when she moved. She felt so feminine and pretty, and David's compliments on her appearance were adding to her euphoria.

"That's a very attractive ring you're wearing," David said. "Opal, isn't it?"

"Yes. It was a gift from my grandfather Robert," Patty said. "I couldn't wear it while I was pregnant with Sophia because my fingers were rather puffy." She splayed her hand in front of her. "See how it changes colors in the candlelight? There are so many facets to it, much more depth than is visible at first glance."

Just like Patty herself, David thought. Yes, just like Patty.

Their dinners were set in front of them and they ate in silence for several minutes.

"This is so delicious," Patty said, smiling. "I just hope I don't forget and start clearing the table when we're finished."

David chuckled. "There you go." He paused. "Did your grandfather give you that ring for a special occasion? I don't mean to be harping on the ring, but it really is exquisite."

"Robert MacAllister gave each of his grandchildren a gift that he very carefully selected just for them," Patty said. "My father and Ryan MacAllister were partners on the police force for years and Sharpes have always been considered members of the MacAllister family. To Robert, my brother and I were two more of his granddchildren. None of us knew what we were getting, or when it would be our turn. Most of the presents were actually a message to the recipient."

"A message?"

Patty nodded. "I know the message of some of the gifts, but not everyone chose to share it."

"Fascinating. Can you give me an example?"

"Well, I don't think Ryan would mind if I told you this. He had struggled for many years to find his place because of his mixed heritage. My grandfather gave him a beautiful antique globe that made Ryan realize that he didn't have to choose one of his cultures over the other, that he could embrace both of his worlds. It was a major turning point in my brother's life."

"Your grandfather sounds like a wise and wonderful man," David said. "So, what's the message you received from that ring?"

"Oh, there isn't one," Patty said.

"Are you certain of that?"

Patty glanced at the ring again. "Well, yes. I can remember staring and staring at it, then coming to the conclusion that it was simply a gorgeous piece of jewelry that was selected just for me because my grandfather knew I would cherish it. There's no message, though."

David leaned toward her slightly. "Patty, you just told me what the message is."

"What?"

"You said that the ring changes colors, has much more depth and facets than are visible at first glance. You could have been talking about you, not the ring."

Patty laughed. "You're contradicting yourself, David. You're the one who finally realized that I'm exactly what I present myself to be. Nothing hidden, nothing beyond what you see is what you get."

"No, I'm *not* contradicting myself. Yes, you're

honest and real and who you present yourself to be. But a person needs time, which I have had, to discover and appreciate all the facets of you, the depth of who you are. Just like the ring.''

''Why, David Montgomery,'' Patty said, smiling at him warmly, ''you are a romantic. You want there to be a special message connected to this ring, just as there was something Ryan needed to know that he found out when he received the globe. But the ring? No. No hidden meaning. You're blowing your image of being an I-always-deal-in-clear-cut-facts attorney, sir.''

''And you're flunking being a whimsical princess,'' David said, chuckling.

''That's because princesses don't change diapers and wipe sticky jelly from little fingers.''

''You've got a point there,'' David said, nodding. ''But then again…''

''Enough,'' she said. ''I'm going to clean my plate like a good little girl so I can have one of those sinful desserts I saw going by on the cart the waiter is pushing. And to prove that I can be whimsical, I hereby declare there are no calories in any of those yummy creations. The cheesecake with the dark cherries on top is calling my name.''

''Then it shall be yours, Princess Patty. Your wish is my command.''

Then I wish that this night would never end, Patty thought dreamily. It was so perfect and she was having such carefree fun while in the company of a magnificent man who loved her. Oh, yes, this night was creating memories to keep forever.

* * *

Several hours later Patty lay in bed, smiling into the darkness as she relived each moment of the evening with David.

They had lingered over coffee and the coveted cheesecake, then finally left the restaurant to stroll through a pretty garden behind it. When they returned to the house, the sitter had a glowing report about the children, then David had paid the woman and driven her home.

When he came back to the house they had made love, soared to their special and private place, then lay close together to savor the sensations still rippling throughout them.

David had left the bed with grumbling reluctance, dressed, then carried a sleeping Sarah Ann out the front door. Patty had smiled and waved as they drove away. She had continued to smile as she washed her face and brushed her teeth, donned her nightshirt and crawled back into the bed.

And she was still smiling as she indulged in a minute-by-minute reflection of the past hours.

"Oh, my," she said, wiggling into a comfortable position. "Heavenly."

But how long would David be satisfied with this arrangement? she thought in the next instant, her smile fading. Getting dressed and going home to that big house was not what he wanted. He envisioned a family under that roof, all of them together, with her as his wife. And that wasn't going to happen.

Don't go there, Patty told herself. Not tonight. She didn't want to do one thing to diminish the pleasure of the time spent with David.

She rolled onto her side and slid one hand under

the pillow, the other beneath her cheek, then frowned as she felt a prick on her soft skin.

The ring, she thought, sitting up and snapping on the lamp. She'd forgotten to take off the opal ring.

She slipped it from her finger and started to place it on the nightstand, only to hesitate and hold it before her with the fingertips of both hands. She tilted it this way, then that, seeing the changing colors in the glow of the lamp.

David was convinced, she mused, that there *was* a message connected to the ring. He was certain that her grandfather was attempting to show her that *she* had many facets and a greater depth of self than she perceived she had.

Could that possibly be true? Had she somehow sold herself short? Had she, when Peter left her, automatically assumed the guilt of his leaving, labeled herself a failure as a wife because he had gone to another woman to fulfill his needs? Had she then focused on her role of mother because it was safe there, the evidence of her expertise in that arena evident each day in her children?

Patty moved the ring back and forth again.

Many facets, she thought. Depths not visible at first glimpse. She had allowed herself to reach for one of those depths when she separated the mother from the woman when she was alone with David. Yes, she had done that and it felt right, the way it should be.

But the next layer? The wife? No, there was nothing further to discover about being a wife. If she hadn't failed in that role Peter wouldn't have left her. Nothing was going to change the truth of that.

But...

Maybe, just maybe, she could gain some inner peace about it if she knew how she had failed him. He had never told her what her shortcomings had been. He'd simply announced that he was in love with another woman and was ending his marriage to Patty. He had been so completely unhappy in their union that he didn't even visit the children they had created together.

Knowing what she had done wrong would not change things between her and David, she thought. Hearing the stark list of her inadequacies didn't mean she had the capability to do things differently with someone else. No, she would still hold fast to her vow never to marry again.

But if she could say to herself "I was a failure as a wife because…" it might be easier to deal with, give her a better understanding of who she was, be a growing experience that would be beneficial to the woman she'd allowed to surface.

Patty nodded, then placed the ring on the nightstand. She turned off the light, then settled again, shifting her mind back to the memories of the evening spent with David.

David threw back the blankets on the bed and got to his feet.

Damn it, he thought as he left the bedroom. He couldn't sleep, and tossing and turning was even difficult because of the cast on his leg. Orange juice. He'd have a glass of the ever-famous orange juice, then try again to relax in bed.

His bed. His empty, lonely bed that he should be

sharing with Patty Clark but wasn't, and the way things stood, never would.

In the kitchen David sank onto a chair at the table with the drink he really didn't want and glowered at the far wall.

The evening he'd just spent with Patty had been great, really super, so nice. She had looked like the beautiful princess he'd declared her to be and her eyes had sparkled each time she smiled and... Oh, yes, those had been very special, memory-making hours.

And then?

David drained the glass and slammed it onto the table.

And then reality check, Montgomery. He'd hauled himself out of Patty's warm embrace and the comfort of her bed, collected his sleeping daughter, and left the house like a thief in the night.

The memory of *that* portion of the evening was rapidly diminishing the glow—for lack of a better word—of the time spent at the restaurant, then the lovemaking shared.

"Hell," David said, his shoulders slumping.

The thought of evenings with Patty far into the future ending as this one had was depressing beyond belief. She was offering him a mere crumb of the cake representing his existence. Crumb of the cake? How corny was that? Geez. But he knew what he meant and he also knew it wasn't going to be enough.

He wanted it all, greedy so-and-so that he was. A wife for him. A mother for Sarah Ann. This big empty house filled to the brim with love and laughter and so many kids they'd have to wear name tags to keep them all straight.

He wanted Patty next to him when he fell asleep at night and there when he woke in the morning. He'd walk in the door at the end of a workday and smell the aroma of dinner cooking. Then he'd open his arms to children who were so glad to see their daddy arrive home, and smile at Patty over their heads, sending and receiving the message of love.

Message. Patty's opal ring. If *he* could figure out the message of the ring that Robert MacAllister intended Patty to discover, then Patty sure as hell could because it was *her* grandfather and *her* ring.

She'd convinced herself there was no message because she was too frightened to embrace it. It was easier to label herself a failure as a wife and vow never to marry again than to listen to the ring whisper to her that she was hiding behind Peter's betrayal rather than run the risk of once again being a wife.

Patty refused to budge on the subject of how far their relationship could and would go, had set down the rules, offered him the crumb, and that was that.

And it wasn't enough.

It was too empty, too chilling, too lonely.

Oh, yeah, he'd been determined to fight the battle, win the war, declare himself the victor, then marry Patty Clark.

But that wasn't going to happen. He knew that now. Tonight had been the blueprint for how things were going to be and he hated it.

"Ah, Patty," David said, his voice ringing with emotion. "We could have had it all, don't you see, because we love each other and..." An achy sensation in his throat choked off David's words and he shook his head. "But the crumb just isn't enough. Not enough. I can't do this." He drew a shuddering breath. "It's over."

The next morning an exhausted-from-lack-of-sleep David telephoned Patty and asked if she would meet him at the park near her house at three-thirty, which would allow for the completion of nap time. By providing somewhere for Sarah Ann and Tucker to play, he and Patty could have a private conversation.

"About what?" Patty said, a chilling sense of foreboding sweeping through her.

"I'll tell you when I see you."

"Well, yes, okay," she said, her hold on the receiver tightening. "Are you all right, David? You sound...strange."

"I'm just tired. I didn't sleep well last night. Three-thirty. Goodbye, Patty."

"'Bye," she said, then replaced the receiver slowly, while having the irrational thought that she wished she had not answered the ringing phone.

The dread that had settled over Patty after talking to David did not diminish as the hours until their rendezvous dragged slowly by.

At three-thirty she parked next to David's SUV in the lot at the park, then helped Tucker from the car. She settled Sophia in the stroller and the trio started down the cobblestone path leading to the playground area.

"There's Sarah Ann," Tucker yelled. "See her, Mommy? She's in the sandbox waiting for me. Can I run, run, run?"

Patty smiled. "Yes, you may run, run, run. But

remember, Tucker, you're not to pretend that the sand is snow and pour it over your head."

"'Kay," he said, then dashed toward a waving Sarah Ann.

Patty watched him go, then swept her gaze over the benches surrounding the playground, seeing David rise and start in her direction.

He isn't smiling, Patty thought, registering a steadily increasing sense of panic. She was going to snatch Tucker out of the sandbox and hightail it home before David could tell her what was on his mind.

He was coming closer and closer. He looked so tired, had dark circles beneath those mesmerizing blue eyes of his, and he was limping more than usual, as though he didn't have the energy to swing the cast on his leg forward with each step that was bringing him closer and closer.

Patty could hear the echo in her ears of her own wildly beating heart when David stopped next to Sophia's stroller, a frown on his face.

"Hello, David," Patty said, attempting to produce a cheery tone of voice that didn't quite materialize.

"Patty," he said, nodding slightly. "Shall we sit down?"

They settled onto a bench that gave them a clear view of Sarah Ann and Tucker, yet was too far away from the children for them to hear what was being said by the adults. Patty pulled the stroller around so she could see Sophia who was happily blowing bubbles from between her tiny lips.

"Sophia is really into bubble-blowing," Patty said. "I have no idea why, but she thinks it's great fun. She's extremely intelligent, of course, to be able to do that at such a young age. I wish she'd come up with a new game, though, because that bubble-blowing is chapping her chin and…"

"Patty," David said quietly, shifting on the bench to look directly at her.

"I don't want to hear what you have to say, David," she said, her voice quivering. "I could tell by the tone of your voice on the telephone that something was terribly wrong and now that I see you I know that I'm right, and I just don't want to deal with…" Patty stopped speaking and sighed. "You're ending things between us, aren't you?"

"I have to," David said. "Last night was a very clear picture of how things would go under your rules, or whatever you want to call them. I can't live that way, Patty. I don't want to drive home in the dead of night my child sleeping in the back seat of my vehicle. I don't want to wake up the next morning alone in my bed.

"I want to marry you, live under the same roof with you, be able to reach for you in the night and know that you're sleeping beside me. I want all of us to be a family, a real family, living, laughing, loving, having hopes and dreams and goals for the future that we plan together."

"David—"

"That's what *I* want," he said, "but it's not what *you* want. Oh, I could play ostrich and pretend that maybe it isn't true, maybe you'll change your mind-set about becoming my wife. If I did that I could continue to see you, be with you. But it wouldn't be fair to Sarah Ann to allow her to believe that being with you, Tucker and Sophia is the way things will always be, then yank the rug out from beneath her later. I can't do that to her.

"Patty, I love you so much," David said, his voice growing raspy with emotion. "But what you're willing to give in this relationship isn't enough. It just isn't. An ongoing affair is too shallow, empty, lonely. I can't do this."

Tears misted Patty eyes. "I've failed you, haven't I? I can't meet your needs, give you what you want, and so you're leaving me."

"Don't start comparing me to Peter," David said, a pulse ticking in his temple. "You think you failed him as a wife and he left you. You think you failed me as a lover and I'm leaving you."

"Well, it's true," she said, two tears spilling onto her pale cheeks. "You're ending things between us and it's all my fault."

"No, damn it, it isn't all your fault," David said, his voice rising. "I could say that *I* failed *you* because I wasn't capable of meeting *your* needs, accepting you, the woman I love, on your terms. But there's no blame to be placed here. We just can't connect on the last piece of the puzzle. Everything else is great, perfect, wonderful, but…

"God, Patty, I don't want to end what we have together. The thought of never seeing you again, never holding you, making love with you, hearing your laughter, watching those eyes of yours sparkle when you… The mere image in my mind of walking out of your life is ripping me to shreds."

Patty pressed trembling fingertips to her lips to stifle a sob.

"But to postpone it," David went on, "will just

make it worse down the road. It's better to make a clean break now.''

He shook his head. ''This is so damn hard. I envisioned seeing Sophia's first smile, her first wobbling steps, hear her first words—that would include her calling me Daddy—and I was going to play ball with Tucker, you know? Get him a little baseball glove and a bat and...

''Hell, there's no reason why I couldn't teach Sarah Ann to play ball, too. We'd be out in the yard playing, then you'd call us in for dinner and we'd sit around the table as a family. Man, I'm killing myself here saying all this stuff that is never going to happen.''

''I'm sorry, David,'' Patty said, crying openly. ''I'm just so very sorry that I couldn't give you what you need to be happy.''

''And I'm very sorry that I couldn't make what you were capable of giving me be enough. We were close, so close to having it all. So close, yet so very far apart.'' David got to his feet and stood staring at Sophia for a long moment before switching his gaze back to Patty. ''I've got to go now. There's no point in dragging this out any longer. I'll get Sarah Ann. Patty, I love you. I only wish this weren't goodbye. I really hate that word right now. But goodbye.''

Through a blur of tears, Patty watched David lift a complaining Sarah Ann from the sandbox, then leave the park. She heard his vehicle start, then the sound of the powerful engine grew fainter and fainter until it finally disappeared.

Patty wrapped her hands around her elbows and struggled for emotional control, not wishing to upset Tucker with her crying.

David, her mind screamed. *Don't leave me, please, David. I love you. I love you so much. I'm so sorry I failed you. Oh, God, David, please don't...*

It's too late, she thought. David was gone. All that they'd had together, everything they'd shared, was over. She was alone and she had no one to blame but herself. She'd hurt David. She was the source of his pain and so he had left her.

There was no wondering why he had walked out of her life, no mystery to his leaving as there was with Peter. David Montgomery wanted a wife and she didn't know how to be a proper wife. End of story. The beginning of so many long and lonely nights that would stretch into infinity.

Tucker left the sandbox and ran toward Patty, causing her to quickly dash the tears from her cheeks and produce a smile by the time he arrived in front of her.

"Hi, big boy," she said. "Having fun?"

"I was, but David tooked Sarah Ann home already." Tucker cocked his head to one side and stared at Patty. "You look funny, Mommy. Your face is really white and your nose is really red."

"Allergies," Patty said. "Something is in bloom here in the park that is causing my allergies to go cuckoo. It's nothing to worry about."

"I guess David gots allergies, too, 'cause his voice was weird when he said 'bye to me and told me to give you a hug from him. Why didn't he give you a hug himself?"

"That's just something grown-ups say sometimes when they're leaving," Patty said. "I can push Sophia's stroller over by the swings and push you as high as the sky. Would you like that?"

"Yes," Tucker yelled. "You're the bestis mom in the whole wide world."

Patty stood and started to push the stroller toward the swings as Tucker ran on ahead.

Oh, yes, she thought, struggling against fresh tears, as a mommy she was top-notch. An Olympic Gold mother. And as a woman making love with the man of her heart? She had given herself in total, trusting abandon and welcomed and received all that he had brought to her.

But David wanted more.

David wanted a wife.

But she couldn't give him what he wanted.

So David was gone.

And her heart was shattering into a million pieces.

Patty drew a shuddering breath as she parked the stroller and began to push Tucker on the swing.

The only hope she had of gaining even a modicum of inner peace, she thought, was to know why, how, her flaw had destroyed her marriage to Peter and robbed her of a future with David.

There was only one person who possessed the answers she needed. She'd have to gather every ounce of inner strength she could muster to have the fortitude to hear the actual words spoken, listen to the list of her failings but she had to do it.

After all these months she would have to meet with Peter.

Chapter Fifteen

Late the next morning Patty paced restlessly across her living room, alternating between wringing her hands and wrapping them around her elbows. She was dressed in trim, dark-blue slacks and a lighter blue string sweater, and her freshly shampooed hair fell back into place each time she turned her head as she retraced her steps.

"Patty," Hannah Sharpe said, watching her daughter's performance. "You're making me dizzy. You're terribly tense for someone who asked me to babysit so you could run some errands. And why do you keep looking at your watch? A person doesn't make an appointment to do errands as far as I know. Are you ready to tell me what's really going on?"

Patty halted her trek and looked at her mother.

"I'm meeting Peter for lunch at a café near his

office,'' she blurted out in a rush of words, then drew a much-needed breath.

"Peter?" Hannah said, her eyes widening. "Why on earth would you want to see that man? Honey, he hasn't bothered to visit Tucker in months, and he never acknowledged Sophia's birth and… No, Hannah, hush. I will *not* be an interfering mother."

"I have to talk to him about something that is important to me." Patty fiddled with the opal ring she had slipped on her finger. "I'm telling myself that this ring from Grandpa will give me the courage to get through this, but I don't think the butterflies in my stomach understand the plan." She looked at her watch again. "I've got to go. Thank you for watching the kids."

"You know that's never a problem," Hannah said. "Your father and your Uncle Ryan are coming by here to pick up Tucker and take him to a petting zoo that's set up in the parking lot of the mall. Sophia and I will be fine so there's no need for you to rush back. But I can't imagine why you're going in the first place. It would make sense if you said you were meeting David for lunch."

"No, it wouldn't," Patty said miserably. "Believe me, Mother, it wouldn't." She paused. "Tucker? Will you come kiss Mommy goodbye? I'm leaving now."

Tucker came running from his room, gave Patty a smacking kiss on the cheek, then said he had to finish the picture he was coloring for his grandma and dashed back down the hallway.

"It's just breaking his little heart that I'm going off without him," Patty said, rolling her eyes heavenward. "Well. Here I go. Yes." She snatched her purse from one of the chairs. "Goodbye, Patty. No, that's not right. *I'm* Patty. Goodbye, Mother."

Hannah frowned. "I'm not certain you should be behind the wheel of your car."

"I'm fine, I'm fine, I'm fine," Patty said, starting toward the front door. "I have to do this, Mom."

"All right, sweetheart."

"'Bye."

During the drive to the restaurant, Patty mentally lectured herself to get a grip, gain control, be prepared to appear calm, cool and collected when she saw her ex-husband for the first time in months.

Peter would not have a clue about how difficult it was to be near him, reliving the pain of his betrayal. But she was on a fact-finding mission and was determined to get the information she sought. It just happened to be Peter Clark who knew what she needed to know. No big deal. She could handle this. Yeah, right.

Patty parked in the lot next to the small café, locked her car, straightened her shoulders and marched into the restaurant, totally ignoring the trembling in her legs and the increased swirl of the butterflies in her stomach.

She stopped just inside the door and glanced around. Peter slid out of a booth in the far corner and raised one hand to gain Patty's attention.

With each step she took toward Peter, Patty felt the butterflies quiet their frenzied flight and her legs cease the maddening trembling.

There was Peter, she thought. The father of her children, the man she had vowed to spend the remainder of her days with. There was Peter. A stranger to her now. Someone who no longer had the ability to hurt her because she felt nothing for him. Nothing.

"Hello, Patty," Peter said quietly, when she reached the booth.

"Peter," she said, then slid onto the bench seat.

He sat down opposite her.

"You look fantastic," he said, managing to produce a small smile.

"Thank you." Patty lifted her chin. "I must say, Peter, you aren't looking well at all. You've lost weight. Have you been ill?"

"No, not really," Peter said. "I've just been under a great deal of stress during the past few months."

"Oh."

"Ready to order?" a waitress said pleasantly, as she appeared at the edge of the table.

Patty asked for a chicken salad and Peter ordered a hamburger and fries. The waitress nodded and hurried away.

"How are the kids?" Peter said.

"I don't believe you have the right to ask that question," Patty said. "You don't even know what I named our—my—daughter. I refuse to give you an update on how the children are, Peter. You can insist, I suppose, since you pay child support but I doubt that you sincerely care how they are."

"You've changed," Peter said, narrowing his eyes. "You're—I don't know what word I want—tougher? Stronger?"

"I've grown up a great deal since you left," Patty said, one fingertip stroking the opal stone in the ring. *"Tougher? Stronger?.* Yes, those words apply, as does *more mature*. I'm no longer someone who is willing to accept quietly whatever might be done to her. I am now a woman who is fully prepared to raise her children and take care of them, as well as herself.''

''I've heard that you're seeing someone,'' Peter said.

''That's none of your business.''

''Chicken salad,'' the waitress said, sliding a plate in front of Patty. ''Burger,'' she added, plunking down Peter's lunch. ''Drinks?''

''No, this water is fine,'' Patty said. ''Thank you.''

''Same for me,'' Peter said.

''Okeydokey,'' the woman said, then disappeared again.

Patty picked up her fork, stared at the salad, then set the fork on the edge of the plate.

''I'm going to ask you something, Peter,'' she said, ''and I'd like an honest answer. You owe me that much.''

''All right. What's the question?''

Oh, God, Patty thought, she couldn't do this. She didn't want to hear the words that would chip away at her, piece by piece, as Peter listed her sins, the ways she had failed him as a wife. No.

Yes. She had to do this. Peter's answer could be a slender, fragile thread to possible inner peace. It could give her the ability to accept herself as she was once she knew the definition of her failure.

''I...I would like you to tell me,'' she said, wishing her voice didn't sound so shaky, ''how I failed you as a wife. I realize that I didn't make you happy, wasn't capable of being for you what you wanted and needed me to be, but you never told me where I had gone wrong, what I had done to drive you into the arms of another woman. I have the right to know, Peter, and I want the truth. How did I fail you?''

Peter opened his mouth to speak, then snapped it closed. His shoulders slumped and he dropped his chin to his chest. Seconds ticked by before he looked at Patty again, and her breath caught when she saw the tears glistening in his eyes.

''Oh, Patty,'' he said. ''You didn't fail me as a wife, or woman, or the mother of my son. You are *not* a failure. I am. You are everything and more than any man could ever hope to find in all those roles.''

''What?'' she whispered.

''It was me, don't you understand? I was the rising star of the company. I had the golden touch. I wrote more insurance policies than anyone else, left the other salesmen in the dust. The bosses were talking about giving me a bigger office, a hefty raise, hinted at stock options being the next step for me up my ladder to shining success. I soaked it all up like a thirsty sponge, strutted my stuff, was so full of self-importance.

''Then I'd come home at night to our little house and you'd have dinner ready and Tucker would run to greet me, and I knew the evening would consist of playing with him, then watching TV with you until it was time for us to go to bed.''

Patty frowned as she nodded.

''It was suddenly too ordinary, too dull for me, the wonder kid. I deserved more than a cookie-cutter house, meat loaf and mashed potatoes and a docile little wife who wanted nothing more than to please me. I had earned some excitement, by God, some sizzle, party time, nights on the town. You were a dedicated wife and mother and I didn't want to settle for that.''

"Dear heaven," Patty said.

"And whoa," he went on, "look at this. Here was my sexy secretary suddenly making it clear that she liked my new status at the office, wanted to be in on the fun and games that went with my clout and bigger paycheck. Gloria was ready to party and so was I. I actually convinced myself that I had fallen in love with her and wanted the world that came with being with her.''

"And so you walked away from me, our marriage, our son, the new baby that was on the way," Patty said, struggling against threatening tears. "Without a backward glance, you went.''

"Yes."

"But—"

"Listen to me," Peter said, reaching over and gripping one of her hands. "You did not fail me as a wife. I swear to God, Patty, you didn't. I was the luckiest man in the world to have your love and devotion and I was too stupid to realize it until it was too late. I quit coming to visit Tucker because I didn't deserve to hear him call me Daddy. I didn't acknowledge the new baby for the same reason. The least I could do for you, for our children, was to stay out of your lives.''

"I thought...I thought it was my fault that you—"

"No, no, never," he said, releasing her hand and slouching back in the booth. "It was me, all me. And

Gloria? When I started suggesting that we stay home more, spend quiet evenings watching TV, cook dinner there, she sent me packing and went to work for another company. I haven't seen her in months.''

"I had no idea," Patty said.

"*I* destroyed our marriage, Patty," Peter said, his voice thick with emotion. "And I didn't even entertain the idea of begging you to forgive me because I didn't deserve to be forgiven. I'm leaving next month to head up the office in Kansas City. It's the only thing that I have left to give you and our children— to have me permanently out of your lives so you can move forward, all of you.

"But, Patty? Don't ever doubt yourself as a wife, a woman, a mother. Please, don't do that. If this man you're seeing deserves you, then he already knows how damn lucky he is that you're a part of his life.

"Don't let what I did to you stop you from being happy, having everything I wasn't capable of giving you. Just be you. When you're with that man, just be you, and if he's smart he'll spend the rest of his life thanking God that you chose him to be the recipient of the kind of love you give so freely.''

"Oh, Peter, I don't know what to say."

Peter dug in his pocket, then tossed some bills on the table. He slid out of the booth and met Patty's gaze.

"Don't say anything," he said. "Just be happy. I'm so damn sorry for what I did. Follow your heart. Just be you."

Peter strode away, and Patty pressed her fingertips to her lips and closed her eyes for a long moment. She opened them again and stared at the opal ring on her finger, her mind racing with all that Peter had divulged to her.

She turned her hand slowly to the left, seeing the colors of the opal shimmering in the light.

Woman, she thought, then tipped her hand in the opposite direction, bringing new shades for her to see. Mother.

With a smile slowly forming on her lips she lifted her hand directly in front of her, producing yet another facet of the beautiful ring.

Wife, her heart sang. Oh, Grandpa, thank you. There *was* a message connected to Robert Mac-Allister's gift. She had just been far, far too frightened to listen to the whispers from the ring.

As Patty slid out of the booth, the waitress rushed to her side.

"Is something wrong?" the woman said, glancing at the table. "You and your friend didn't even touch your meals."

"Oh, no," Patty said, smiling. "Nothing is wrong. In fact, for the first time in a very long while, everything is very, very right."

The waitress shrugged. "Okeydokey."

As Patty drove across town she ordered the butterflies that were threatening to return to hit the road. She was well aware of the importance of what she was about to do and needed all her courage. The rest of her life, her future happiness, was going to be determined at her destination, and there was no room for shaky nerves or trembling knees.

"I am woman," Patty said aloud. "I am mother.

And, oh, David, if you can forgive me for being such a frightened child, then *I am wife.*''

A rush of relief swept through Patty when she saw David's SUV parked at his house. She could only hope that he was following the plan of taking Sarah Ann to the Fuzzy Bunny while he finished unpacking, then having the new housekeeper come in later so he could begin to look for office space.

Not allowing herself to think how far it was from her vehicle to the front door, Patty turned off the ignition and got out of the car. She drew one steadying breath, then hurried to the front door, pressing the doorbell when she arrived.

''Yeah. Coming. Hang on,'' David yelled from inside the house.

Hurry, David, Patty thought, before I faint dead out on my face.

The door opened and David appeared with a stack of books in his arms, his chin resting on the top volume.

''Patty?'' His shock at seeing her caused him to lose control of the teetering tower of books and they fell crashing to the floor. ''Hell.''

''I'm sorry,'' Patty said. ''I obviously should have called first. I'll help you pick up the books.''

''Forget the books,'' he said. ''Come in. Just step over this mess. Why are you here?''

Patty entered the house and David scooped the books to the side to allow him to close the door behind her. He looked at her questioningly.

''May I sit down?'' she said.

''Oh, sure. Sure.'' He swept one arm in the direction of the living room.

Patty sank gratefully onto the sofa and David settled onto a large barrel chair across from her.

"Is Sarah Ann at the Fuzzy Bunny?" Patty said.

David nodded.

"Good, because I need to speak to you privately, with no interruptions."

"I'm listening," David said.

Patty stared at the opal ring for a long moment, slid one fingertip over the stone, then met David's gaze again.

"David, you were right. There was a message connected to this ring, but I was just too frightened to listen to it, believe in it. There *are* many facets to me, depths I didn't have the courage to embrace any longer because I believed that I had failed Peter as a wife and would always be a failure as a wife.

"But I just met with Peter and I finally know the truth. He assured me that I didn't fail him, that he was the one who fell short in his role of husband, man, father. I should have believed in myself all along but I was just so devastated by what Peter had done that I..." She shook her head.

"Go on," David urged.

"I'm like this opal," Patty said, sudden tears misting her eyes. "I have many facets, depths, that I now know are mine to own, to glory in. I am a woman. I am a mother. And, oh, God, David, if I'm not too late, if your proposal still stands, if you can forgive me for hurting you, then..."

A sob caught in Patty's throat. "...then I will also be a wife. *Your* wife. I love you so much, David. I'm so sorry for the pain I caused you, but if you can put all that behind you and… Please, David? Will…will you marry me?''

David moved so fast that a gasp escaped from Patty's lips. He closed the distance between them, hauled her up into his arms and kissed her so passionately she was convinced her bones were dissolving. When he finally raised his head, they both drew shuddering breaths.

"I thought I'd lost you forever," he said, his voice raspy. "I thought… Oh, thank God, you listened to the message from the ring. Patty, I love you, will always love you. Yes, Patty Clark, I will marry you.

"We *are* going to have it all. We'll be a family, here in this house that will be a home filled with love and laughter. If we're blessed with another daughter I want her middle name to be Opal. Hell, if we have a boy, *his* middle name will be Opal. That ring opened the tightly closed door to our future together. Oh, how I love you."

"And I love you, David Montgomery," Patty said, smiling through tears of joy. "Goodness, wait until Tucker and Sarah Ann learn they're to be officially brother and sister. They'll be so excited."

David smiled. "We'll tell everyone, the world, that we're going to be married. But before we go nuts with our big announcement, there's something I want to do."

"Make love to me?" Patty said, raising her eyebrows.

"Oh, yes, ma'am, that is definitely on the agenda." David paused. "But this is something else. I'd like to go see Robert MacAllister and shake his hand, thank him from my heart for being so wise, for loving you enough to give you the opal ring.''

''That's wonderful,'' Patty said. ''*You're* wonderful. Visiting my grandfather will be the first step on the path that represents our journey into the future... together.''

Silhouette®

SPECIAL EDITION™

From reader favorite

Christine Flynn
PRODIGAL PRINCE CHARMING

(Silhouette Special Edition #1624)

International playboy Cord Kendrick didn't need *another* scandal to bring on the disapproval of his family. So when he accidentally destroyed Madison O'Malley's business, he offered to do whatever it took to make it up to her. But the more time he spent with the sexy chef, the more he wanted her. Could he convince the skeptical beauty that his feelings were for real?

Don't miss this last story about Virginia's most prominent political family!

The KENDRICKS *of* CAMELOT

Public lives...private loves.

Available July 2004 at your favorite retail outlet.

If you enjoyed what you just read,
then we've got an offer you can't resist!

Take 2 bestselling
love stories FREE!
Plus get a FREE surprise gift!

SILHOUETTE

SPECIAL EDITION™

From bestselling author

Victoria Pade

BABIES IN THE BARGAIN

(Silhouette Special Edition #1623)

A sexy cop left alone to raise his twin girls
accepts the help of his daughters' blond
bombshell aunt as temporary nanny.
Before long, serious sparks begin to fly,
wreaking havoc on their platonic relationship
and causing fantasies about a new and
improved happily-ever-after....

Northbridge Nuptials

Where a walk down the aisle is never far behind.

*Available July 2004
at your favorite retail outlet.*

Silhouette®

COMING NEXT MONTH

SPECIAL EDITION

SSECNM0604